D1396383

Give Us the Vote!

Sue Reid

SCHOLASTIC

For Dora's family, and all those who remember her with
affection

ISBN 978 1407 11781 2

All rights reserved
Printed and bound by CPI Bookmarque, Croydon CR0 4TD
Cover image supplied by www.photolibrary.co.uk

2 4 6 8 10 9 7 5 3 1

The right of Sue Reid to be identified as the author of this work has been
asserted by her in accordance with the Copyright, Designs
and Patents Act, 1988.

Chapter One

'Men of Huddersfield. Will you allow the Liberal government to treat the women of this country so unjustly?' The speaker paused for a minute and surveyed her audience. 'This Liberal government, which *says* it supports women's right to vote, refused to listen to them when they went to Parliament to ask for that right. Worse, it flung them into prison for it!' The speaker's voice rose angrily, carrying easily over the crowd to where Dora stood, several rows back.

'That's Mrs Pankhurst,' the woman next to Dora nudged her.

'Aye, I know,' the girl said, gazing raptly up at the slight but commanding figure on top of the wagon. 'I've seen her picture in the papers.' And me mam has gone on about her till she's blue in the face, she could have added. Mrs Pankhurst, the woman who had founded the Women's Social and Political Union, the WSPU, to campaign for women's right to vote. Was there anyone in that crowd who didn't know who she was? Already they – the suffragettes – had made the cause headline news – especially since women had gone to prison for it. Deeds, not words, that was their motto. And about time too, Dora thought. For nearly fifty years women had campaigned peacefully. But where had it got them? Nowhere. To Dora's mind it was quite right that women should have the vote. Women went out to work, paid taxes, raised children and ran the home. If they were fit for that, they were fit to vote too.

But what did they think an' all? The men. Dora looked at the sea of caps surrounding her. It would take a good deal of courage to stand up and address this lot, she thought. Men weren't used to seeing women climb on to wagons to harangue them about their rights – or anything else for that matter. They thought women should stay at home and do what they were told. And as for women getting the vote – most of them thought it was a joke. All they cared about was a tidy house and tea on the table when they got home. How they'd stared when Mrs Pankhurst had first got up on that wagon – eyes out on stalks, jaws dropping. But a lot of them now were nodding their heads thoughtfully, Dora saw, as if they agreed with her – about the prison sentences at least. The harsh sentences handed down to the women had rocked people's sense of fairness. Two months in Holloway they'd got. Two months – merely for demanding the right to vote.

Dora shivered and pulled her shawl more closely round her head and shoulders. It was a raw night, a true Yorkshire

November evening, but she wouldn't have chosen to be anywhere else. How right Mam had been to insist that she came. 'Your life will never be the same again,' she had told her, 'once you've heard Mrs Pankhurst speak.'

She knew why Mrs Pankhurst was there. Mam had explained it to her. Mam knew everything there was to know about the WSPU!

'They've come up to Huddersfield to oppose the Liberal candidate in the by-election,' she told her. The WSPU weren't affiliated to any political party, Dora knew, but they'd made it their policy to oppose every Liberal candidate in every election until the Liberal government honoured their pledge to give women the vote. The by-election had been called in Huddersfield because the Liberal MP had resigned. In the Thewlis family there had been much excitement at the news.

Like most working people the Thewlises were staunch socialists. They hoped that the Labour candidate would win the by-election. And this time there seemed to be a real chance that he would. But, Dora's mother had drummed into her, it was only when *women* got the vote, that their lives would truly get better. Equal rights with men, that's what women wanted.

'It is time to make your feelings known, men,' Dora heard Mrs Pankhurst declaim from the wagon. 'Will you vote for a candidate whose government treats women so brutally? Keep the Liberal out. Vote against the government in the by-election!' She had the crowd in the palm of her hand, Dora thought, as she joined in the applause that thundered out across the square. If she told them to walk up Castle Hill and jump off, they'd do it.

Mrs Pankhurst bowed and climbed down from the wagon. Her place was taken by Mrs Mitchell – one of the WSPU's leaders from over Bolton way and a socialist to boot. 'You've built a fire here in Huddersfield,' she told the crowd in a stirring speech. 'And with your help tonight we'll put a match to it. We'll light such a conflagration that it will never be put out.'

As if the fire had already been lit the audience exploded. Cheers rang across the square. Caps were flung in the air, girls jigged about, arms round each other, smiles lit dour Yorkshire faces. Dora's heart soared. They'd taken one giant step forward tonight. And it was fitting the flame was lit here, in Huddersfield. The WSPU had had its beginnings in the north – in Manchester it was true, a *Lancashire* town, but still a northern one.

'Come on, Dora.' Eliza Thewlis touched her daughter on the arm as the cheers began to subside. 'You heard what Mrs Mitchell said. We're going to speak to them. We're going to offer our help. One woman –' she said, elbowing her way through the crowd to the wagon, 'One woman can do a lot, especially when that woman's Mrs Pankhurst, but she cannot do it all.'

Dora caught her father's eye. He winked. You didn't gainsay Eliza Thewlis when she was in that mood. Mrs T knew her own mind and you did what she asked – or else.

They weren't the only ones hastening up to offer help. There had been a lot of excitement when the news had come that Mrs Pankhurst would be speaking in the town. Though people were beginning to drift away from the square now, a small group of women still hung around the wagon chattering excitedly. Dora's mother marched her straight into the midst of it. Dora's eyes shone. It was thrilling to be there, to be surrounded by brave and determined women, all inspired like her to fight for the vote. And now she was about to meet the leader of them all! What would she be like, she wondered, as they reached the centre of the group where Mrs Pankhurst stood.

'That was a fine speech, Mrs Pankhurst,' she heard her mother say. Mrs Pankhurst inclined her head graciously. 'This is my daughter,' Dora's mother continued. 'She's only sixteen but she's a doughty fighter.' Dora looked up and straight into Mrs Pankhurst's face. She felt her knees bend as if she ought to curtsey. There was something regal about Mrs Pankhurst. Could anyone have thought that a few minutes earlier this woman had been standing atop a wagon, addressing a crowd of hundreds. Not a hair was out of place, her gloves fitted her hands like a second skin.

'Ever since she was seven my daughter has been a diligent reader of the newspapers and she can hold her own in debate on politics,' she heard her mother say. Dora felt her face grow hot. Sometimes Mam went too far.

'Indeed,' said Mrs Pankhurst, and Dora saw a flicker of interest in the eyes that rested on her. There was a steely look in those eyes, Dora thought. Determined. Ruthless, even. If anyone could win women the vote, Mrs Pankhurst could. But that was not all. Those eyes seemed to be searching hers for something. What was it? A promise? The women's cause before all else. 'Can you promise me that?' Could she promise? Could she put the women's cause first, before everything else? Dora swallowed. It was a lot to ask.

Mrs Pankhurst smiled and turned back to Dora's mother. 'Mrs Thewlis, with you and your daughter fighting for the cause, it will soon be won,' she said. She asked if they'd help distribute leaflets for the WSPU. 'We have made a great beginning,' she said. 'But we need willing volunteers to carry the work forward. Will you help us to spread the word?'

'Aye, we will, and gladly,' Dora's mother said. 'We'll take as many as you have to offer.'

'We were the first to offer help,' she boomed as they walked away, hands full of leaflets. 'Remember that, Dora. The first.' Her voice carried strongly in the evening air.

Dora saw a girl in the group round the wagon turn her head and stare at them. Her hands were full of leaflets too. She caught the girl's eye and they smiled briefly at each other.

'Did you see Mrs Key?' said Eliza as they sauntered across the square to the tram stop. 'You know Mrs Key. Her husband keeps that piano shop off Bradford Road, in Regent Place. She was offering help too. I wouldn't be surprised,' she said thoughtfully, adjusting her hat as a gust of wind blew past, 'if they opened a new branch of the WSPU up here in Huddersfield. What with all the enthusiasm for the cause shown here tonight.'

Forgetting that her hands were full of handbills Dora clutched her mother's arm. 'Wouldn't that be grand, Mam!' she said eagerly. 'Do you really think so?' The leaflets fluttered to the ground.

'Mind what you're doing, Dora. You've dropped some of those leaflets. Yes,' her mother said slowly. 'I really think they might.'

There was a big queue for the tram at the stop and the Thewlises had a long wait before one came along that they were able to squeeze on.

'I hope Flo's got the bairns to bed,' Eliza said.

The tram swung slowly north. As it neared the outskirts of the city, it bore left into Bradford Road where the Thewlises alighted. From here it was a short step to their

7

home in Hawthorne Terrace. It was quite dark now and the gaslight at the end of the street had been lit. They walked down the pathway that ran between Hawthorne and Holly Terrace. As they reached the threshold of no. 29, Eliza Thewlis paused and turned to her husband and daughter. 'Tonight,' she said, and her eyes sparkled in the gaslight. 'Tonight the fight begins in Huddersfield. Votes for women!'

Tonight the fight began! 'Votes for women,' decreed Dora.

Chapter Two

'If only you could have heard her, Evie!' Dora said, dreamily. She pulled her nightgown on over her head. Evie was brushing her hair. She put down the brush and glowered at her sister. If Dora mentioned Mrs Pankhurst one more time she'd throw it at her. 'Can't you talk about anything else!' she exclaimed. It had been all Mrs Pankhurst this, Mrs Pankhurst that, ever since Dora had got back from hearing her speak, down at Market Cross.

She picked up the brush again. 'Ninety-three. Ninety-four,' she counted, pulling the brush vigorously through her long thick hair.

Dora scowled and slipped into the bed she shared with her sister, pulling the sheet up to her chin. It felt icy and she shivered, curling up tightly in her nightgown for warmth.

Be nice if at least one of her sisters felt as strongly about the cause as she did, she thought. Couldn't Evie understand that she had to talk to someone? Equal rights for women. Dora drew a deep breath. 'Evie –' she began.

Evie shook her head at her, still counting.

'Ninetynineonehundred,' she said quickly. 'All done.' Teeth chattering, she put the brush down and padded over to the bed.

Next to the bed a candle flickered. Dora gazed at it. 'Mrs Mitchell said we've lit a fire tonight.' She turned over in bed to face her sister. In the dim light Evie's face was a pale orb.

'There's more to life than the suffragettes,' Evie grumbled.

Dora felt like throwing her pillow at her sister. 'Can't you understand at all why women should have the vote? It's not just about our right to vote, it's about what we can do with it – make our lives better. Make others' lives better,' she said passionately. 'Isn't that a cause worth fighting for?'

'You fight for us,' mumbled Evie. 'You've enough fire in your belly for all of us. And talking of fire, mind that candle or you'll have the house alight.'

'Give me a spark o' nature's fire. That's all the learning I desire,' Dora said. She pillowed her head on her arms. Aye, she had. True fire in her belly. She turned back on to her side and thought about the evening. How wonderful it was to have been amongst people who felt so strongly about the cause. Who understood that there was a whole world out there – a world beyond the mills, and if women got the vote, that world would be theirs for the taking –

even if Evie couldn't see it. Tomorrow, as soon as she had finished work, she'd take an armful of those leaflets Mrs Pankhurst had given them and hand them out around the town. What was it Mam had said? 'We were the first to offer Mrs Pankhurst help. Remember that.' Suddenly a girl's face flickered into Dora's memory – it was the face of the girl she had seen by the wagon, Dora recalled. She wished now that she had gone up to speak to her. There was someone she could have talked to, who'd feel like her about the cause. But there'd be others. There had been quite a crowd. Dora smiled sleepily. Aye, there'd be others. They had begun something in Huddersfield this night. Something marvellous. Wax had begun to drip from the candle on to the table. Dora leant across the bed and hastily blew the candle out.

Chapter Three

'Votes for women!' Dora said, smiling as a woman walked past the table holding a young girl's hand. She held a leaflet out to them encouragingly. 'Would you like to read this?' she said. The girl reached out her hand to take it but the woman swatted it away.

'Votes for women, I don't think so,' Dora heard her say tartly.

Dora bristled. 'Your daughter isn't a doll,' she felt like shouting after her. 'She has a mind of her own! Let her use it.' But Dora knew all too well that many women as well as men thought that women shouldn't have the vote.

Still, it was a heady time. The very air felt charged with excitement and she, Dora, was part of it. Sometimes she felt as if she was living a dream. How swiftly life could change, she thought. One minute life was all about standing in front of a weaving loom, ten hours at a stretch, day in day out, like thousands of other girls. But each evening now as soon as work was done she'd hurry into town, chalk suffragette slogans on the pavement, hand out leaflets, and today here she was minding a table piled high with handbills, doing her bit. Mrs Pankhurst said that the Liberal candidate was afraid he'd lose, and it certainly looked that way. Dora had seen him wandering around, sporting white suffragette buttons in his jacket. He'd even come up to the table to speak to her, giving her an oily smile as he tried to reassure her that his government would of course grant women the vote. It was only a matter of time. He'd made sure to say it when there had been plenty around the table to hear him, Dora had noticed. But there had been nervousness behind that false smile. They'd got him on the hop all right. And a good thing too. All those Liberals were about was broken promises.

She was right in the heart of the city here, near the old cloth hall, where the business of buying and selling cloth used to be carried out. She was proud she'd been allowed to help mind the table. Strictly speaking Mam was in charge of it, but Mam had sailed off almost as soon as the suffragettes had set it up. Dora had helped them drape a white WSPU cloth over it, and arranged piles of leaflets on top. The words 'WSPU – VOTES FOR WOMEN' and 'KEEP THE LIBERAL OUT' were stitched on to the cloth in big black letters. No one who read those words could doubt who they were and what they were after. Just as well, Dora thought. There was only a day now to go before the election and all the parties' candidates and their supporters were out, driving around town, plastering the walls with posters. A committee of women textile workers from Lancashire had even turned up and were urging voters to support the Labour candidate.

'Keep the Liberal out.' A woman was bending down to read the words on the cloth. 'Well, I'll go along with that. An' I'll look forward to the day when we women get our rights.'

Dora sat up eagerly. 'Can I give you a leaflet, tell you about the WSPU?'

'No thank you, lass,' the woman said, shaking her head. 'I don't hold with the WSPU's methods.'

Dora leaned forward and said earnestly, 'Aye, but women have been struggling for the vote for more than forty years – and getting nowhere. But that's changing now – thanks to Mrs Pankhurst. She's made women's right to vote headline news. Is that not a step forward?'

'You're getting noticed for the wrong reasons,' said the woman firmly. 'You'll put women's cause back forty years to my mind.'

'If you're treated like outlaws by men, refused the rights men take for granted – the right to vote, the right to a life outside the home, fair pay … then surely you have no choice but to adopt an outlaw's methods.'

A strong voice broke in suddenly. Eliza Thewlis strode up to the table. The woman looked a bit startled. 'Peaceful persuasion has failed,' Eliza said. 'Deeds, not words, that's what's needed now.' She spoke earnestly, as if what the woman thought really mattered to her. 'Maybe if you read what is written here –' Her hands searched among the pamphlets on the table.

'Well, I … I don't rightly know,' the woman said. Eliza pressed a leaflet into her hand.

'Take this home, read it,' she said, 'and if you're not happy with what it says, throw it on the fire. We too hope to light a fire,' she added, 'and by doing so gain what every freeborn person should have. The right to vote!'

'Aye, I will. I will that.' The woman backed away, eyes as round as saucers.

'Oh, Mam!' Dora couldn't help laughing as the woman scuttled away. Her face. It was a study! Her mother settled herself down next to her, and Dora saw her nod approvingly at the handful of leaflets on the table – all that was left of the big pile they'd started with.

'You've done well, Dora,' she said. 'I'm sorry I was so long. I've been down to the Trades Hall, got talking to Mrs Key and some others. There's a lot of interest in starting up a branch here. We've a mind to meet and get things going soon. Mind, we must wait until the election is over and we've seen the Liberal slink off, tail between his legs. And I've no doubt we will. Running scared he is.'

Mam was so confident, Dora thought. She was a powerful speaker too. Look how she'd dealt with that woman. It was only right that she should be able to vote, and she, Dora, would do her utmost to see that she could. She stretched out her legs happily. Wasn't life just grand? A branch of the WSPU in Huddersfield and a Labour MP to represent them in Parliament. What could be better than that?

Chapter Four

'Mam! Mam! 'Ave you heard the news?' Dora hurtled into the room. 'The suffragettes have been released! And they're coming here – to Huddersfield!'

'Mind where you're stepping!' exhorted her mother. Dora stopped her headlong rush and looked down.

Spread on the floor a few inches before her feet was a length of calico. On it was painted in big black letters: 'FIGHT FOR WOMEN'S LIBERTY' and 'KEEP THE LIBERAL OUT'.

'Oh, but it's grand, Mam,' exclaimed Dora, dropping to her knees to take a closer look. Her fingers ran over the ends. 'And haven't you trimmed it nicely.'

'Careful! The letters aren't dry yet,' her mother said.

'I painted them,' chirped up Mabel, from behind her father's chair.

'And you've done it beautifully.' Dora gave her little sister a big kiss.

'What's that paint pot doing on the floor! Move it will you, Dora,' her mother said as a small boy toddled towards it, 'or our Arthur will have it over.'

Dora scooped up the paint pot and put it down on the table just as the small boy reached out his hand for it. Arthur looked at her, lower lip wobbling.

Dora lifted him up hastily and sat down with him, planting him on her knee. 'Now don't you be maungy, Arthur,' she said, giving him a cuddle. 'So what do you think of the news, Father?' she demanded.

'It's grand,' he said, smiling at her. There was a bit of colour in his daughter's cheeks but it wasn't that which made him smile. Dora seemed so alive these days, full of energy. She'd always been passionate about politics but it wasn't just that that had caused a change in her, he felt sure. Hope, he thought suddenly. That was it. She had hope – hope that maybe things were beginning to change for the better for working men and women.

'Aye, the square will be filled to bursting when that train arrives tomorrow,' put in Dora's mother. 'The government will find it made a mistake by releasing the prisoners early.' She turned back to the range, and lifted up the kettle. 'Tea will be ready in a minute. Mabel, you take Arthur and both of you wash your hands. Dora, lass, settle yourself down, take the weight off your feet. You must be exhausted, all that running about.'

It was strange but she didn't feel tired at all, Dora thought as she took her seat at the table. 'Where's the others?' she asked.

'Our Flo is out with her young man. Our Evie...' Her mother shrugged.

Dora helped herself to a slice of bread and spread it with treacle.

'So what time will the train get in?' she asked, taking a mouthful. All that tramping about had made her hungry.

Her parents glanced at each other across the table. Dora caught the look. They were hiding something from her, she thought suspiciously. Something they'd rather not tell her.'

'Three o'clock,' her mother said briskly. 'And,' she went on quickly before Dora could say anything, 'all the halls are booked. Think of that. All of them! They're expecting a grand turnout.'

'Three o'clock, Mam!' Dora burst out. 'Three! But I'll still be at the mill. I'll miss it all.'

'Lass, lass,' her father said gently. 'Don't take on so.'

'We'll keep you a seat,' her mother said.

Dora pushed away her plate and rested her elbows on the table. She didn't feel like eating now. All her hard work – and she'd miss the best moment of all – the moment the released prisoners arrived in town. It wasn't fair. Why must they come at three? she thought furiously. Half the town would still be at work. It didn't make sense. As for Mam keeping her a seat, if they got the turnout Mam thought they would, how would she be able to do that?

She folded her arms and pursed her lips. See if I care, she thought. Let them come.

'We'll be taking the banner,' her father said, breaking the uncomfortable silence. 'And no doubt we'll find another use for it on election night,' he added encouragingly. Dora was silent. There were two spots of angry red in her cheeks. Her father sighed. Best not say any more until she'd simmered down.

Dora felt weary suddenly. 'Mind if I get down?'

Her mother nodded. 'You go on. But mind you're ready for chapel,' she said firmly.

Dora slid off her chair. She could feel her legs ache now – each step felt as if a ball and chain was attached to them. And tomorrow she'd be standing at the loom for ten hours. Ten hours! Suddenly it was all too much. She made a bolt for the staircase and her parents watched as she ran up the stairs.

'Mebbe she'll pick up a book,' said her mother, staring after her. 'Calm her down.'

Her father nodded. Ever since she had been able to read, Dora had been as passionate about books as she was about politics, devouring all the printed matter she could lay her hands on. Books. Newspapers. Wicked it was to his mind that Dora had had to leave school so young to work at the mill. All that promise … wasted at the loom. A door slammed upstairs. Jim's heart felt heavy. He hated to see his daughter so cast down.

Chapter Five

In the weaving shed, the looms were clattering away, like a million knitting needles. It was a wonder she wasn't deaf yet, Dora thought resentfully. She was used to the din but today it grated on her. It just wasn't fair. Here she was, stuck in the mill till half past five. She'd miss it all – not just the excitement of the suffragettes' arrival in the town, but the meeting too. How would she ever get a seat, or find her mam in the crowd? The halls would be packed long before she finished work, whatever Mam said. Even those who weren't sure what they felt about votes for women would be there, eager to hear about the suffragettes' experiences in prison. At dinnertime it was all everyone had talked about.

It was only then, when the looms were stopped, that the weavers were able to have a proper chat. It was impossible to speak or hear what anyone said in the weaving shed. The weavers managed as well as they could by lipreading and hand signals. But they had to be careful that the overlooker didn't see them.

Mabel had brought in the sisters' dinner as usual.

There was never time to go home for it. The girls ate their sandwiches standing up. It was never easy to find a seat. The spinners got to them first and you didn't ask that lot to shift up a bit, make room for them. The spinners reckoned they were a cut above weavers like Dora and her sisters.

What time was it now? Dora pushed a loose strand of hair back off her hot face and tried to concentrate on the piece she was weaving. She mustn't let her thoughts wander, she must keep an eye on the ends, make sure she tied them up quickly and didn't let the threads run on. But it was hard concentrating on her work today.

Three o'clock. The train would be drawing in to the station now. What kind of welcome would they get? The long minutes ticked by. Four o'clock. The suffragettes would be speaking to the crowds now.

Half past five. Time to stop. It was a lot quieter in the weaving shed now, the clatter of the looms replaced by the clatter of clogs. Dora pulled her shawl off the peg where she'd hung it earlier and hurried outside. Her sisters saw her and waved her over. 'Coming home?' Evie asked.

Dora shook her head. 'No – goin' into town. Comin' with me?' she asked, though she knew what the answer would be.

Her sisters shook their heads. 'Come home for tea first,' suggested Evie.

'If I do that, I'll lose any chance of hearing them. I don't want to miss it all.'

'But you'll be too late,' Flora pointed out.

'May as well try,' Dora said.

She waved farewell to her sisters and pushed her way through the crowd shuffling up to the mill gates. Like her a good number turned south. Many would go straight home, reckoning they'd have missed all the excitement, but a few would be keen enough to travel all the way into the centre of town. It was a fair walk from the mill into town though and after standing on her feet all day Dora would have liked to have jumped on a tram, but the only one she could see was barely moving. She could walk faster. The traffic was heavy today.

As Dora hurried down the street, the sound of faint cheers and shouts drifted back to her. Was it them, the suffragettes? Surely not. Not here. The noise grew louder. Dora elbowed her way to the edge of the street and stared down it. The traffic had come to a complete halt. A long line of wagons and carts had been pulled up. Stuck behind them, a motorist tooted his horn impatiently. The wagoner in front shrugged his shoulders. There was nothing he could do. A tram opened its doors and the passengers clambered out into the road. Dora wove her way impatiently round them. She could hear the shouts and cheers clearly now.

She stopped suddenly and blinked. Was she seeing things? A long procession was crossing the road ahead of them, banners flying, sunshine glinting on polished brass. There could be no mistaking who it was. It was them! The suffragettes, followed by half the town it looked like.

'They missed the train,' Dora heard a woman say breathlessly next to her. 'Huddersfield's never seen owt like it – thousands were waiting all afternoon outside the station.' Dora ran down the street. The leaders of the procession were well in sight now.

At the head of the procession strode Christabel Pankhurst arm in arm with Annie Kenney and Mary Gawthorpe. Mary and Annie looked weary, thought Dora, but they held their heads high and their eyes shone. Annie Kenney, one of the WSPU's earliest supporters and now one of its leaders, had been a mill girl herself once, and aged only ten had lost a finger to a flying bobbin in a cotton factory. Mary Gawthorpe was one of the WSPU'S organizers and Yorkshire-born. Both Mary and Annie had recently been released early from Holloway gaol along with the other suffragette prisoners. Dora swallowed. They were so near her now that she could almost have put out a hand and touched Mary's sleeve. Oh, to be part of that glorious procession!

Mary was smiling as she marched past. 'Join us,' she said as the procession swept by. Had Mary Gawthorpe really said that? To her, Dora Thewlis? Or had she imagined it? Well, what of it? Had she not earned a right to be there?

Taking a deep breath, Dora left the crowd on the pavement and slipped into the procession behind Mary and Annie. The woman next to Dora took her arm and linked it with hers.

'Glory, glory hallelujah,' women sang all around her. Dora added her voice to theirs. 'And the cause goes marching on.'

A hundred handkerchiefs fluttered from windows as they passed by. Oh, but it was grand. What would Mam and Dad think if they could see her now?

'For years men have had the vote and what have they done with it?' Dora heard Mrs Pankhurst's voice ring out in the hall as she squeezed in at the back. 'I tell you, it is only when women get the vote that conditions in the factories will change. For years women have fought for their menfolk, for their children. It is time now that they fight for themselves.' Dora felt a lump in her throat. She was glad she hadn't missed this. They needed to hear words like this, factory girls like her, she thought, gazing around at the women and girls in the hall. She couldn't see Mam. The hall was packed – as Mam had forecast it would be. She was lucky to have talked her way in. She looked up at the platform. Mrs Pankhurst's fiery daughter Christabel had begun to speak, leaning forward, both hands on the table. Christabel whom, only a short time earlier, she'd marched behind! She was a wonderful speaker too. Unlike Dora, who had had to leave school when she was twelve, and go to work to help her family, Christabel had had a proper education. She had even got a first-class degree in law, but she could not practise her profession – just because she was a woman. They could not vote for laws, nor could they have any part in making them. One day that would change and then all girls would get the opportunity to study for a degree. And they'd put them to better use than the men had.

There was a roar of applause from the audience. The newly released suffragettes were on their feet. What a time to be alive, Dora thought. Slowly the world was changing. The old certainties were being broken down. In Russia, the autocratic czar had been forced to give the people some form of limited representation. And in New Zealand and in many American and Australian states women had already got the right to vote. If it could happen there – in America and in British colonies at the other end of the world – then surely it could happen here? Everywhere people were rising up, refusing to accept that the world couldn't be a better place – for everyone, not just the few, like the wealthy mill owners.

Chapter Six

Settling back in the chair Dora stretched out her aching legs. When was the last time she'd sat down? She seemed to have been on her feet every blooming minute of every blooming day since the momentous evening when Mrs Pankhurst had descended on the town. The town was bursting with campaigners. She'd caught a glimpse of the suffragettes driving about town on their horse-drawn wagon, handing out leaflets and urging voters to oppose the government that imprisoned women. Sometimes they had climbed down to make speeches. That soon brought eager crowds running up to hear the message: 'Vote against the Liberal.' And tonight the votes would be counted!

What then? Dora wondered. What then? Would the suffragettes depart, their task in Huddersfield finished? Or had Mrs Pankhurst truly started something here?

'Tea's ready!' called Flo from the range. She picked up the kettle and began to pour. 'We'll have it quick and then get down to the polling station,' announced her mother.

The back door opened and Dora's father entered, followed by a young man. 'Evenin' all,' George said cheerily.

Dora glanced at Flo, whose back was to them. Even though there wasn't much light she could swear that her sister's neck had gone pink. She still blushed every time her sweetheart called round and they'd been courting long enough. He was nice, George, thought Dora. Steady. Suited Flo, though a bit too quiet for her taste. Had his own views on what women should be like too.

'We've made the poles for the banner,' her father announced.

Mrs Thewlis gave him a smacking kiss on the cheek. 'It'll look grand down by the station,' she said. 'Now, hurry up all, I promised Annie Kenney we'd not be late.'

My mam promised Annie Kenney we'd not be late! Had her mam really said that? Dora gulped. Mam had told her how Annie had heeded the call, left work to join the WSPU. The overlooker had demanded she return. She hadn't. To think that she, an ordinary mill worker like her, had had the courage to do that. And to go to prison for the cause too. Dora would have liked to talk to her about it. Maybe tonight at the polling station she'd be able to snatch a moment, she thought, hastily draining the last of her tea.

'She'll be there then, Mam?' she said.

'Of course she will. Where else would she be on a night like this,' her mother answered.

'Wasn't she brave – to go to prison for the cause?' Dora said. She caught George's eye and couldn't resist adding mischievously, 'What could be braver than that?'

'There's many sorts of bravery, Dora,' George said quietly. 'My Flo now, she's got lots of pluck, but you wouldn't catch her behaving in such an unladylike way as them suffragettes.'

Dora's eyes flashed. 'They did it because it was the only way to get anyone to sit up and take notice. For years and years suffragettes –'

'Suffragists, Dora, ' her mother corrected her.

'Well yes, the suffragists. The other lot. The Liberal lot. The NUWSS.'

'The posh lot,' put in Evie.

'Yes, the posh lot who think they're too grand for the likes of us. They asked for the vote again and again –'

'Ever so politely,' added her mother.

'Ever so politely,' said Dora.

'But the WSPU are just as posh,' objected George. 'That Mrs Pankhurst and her daughters. Don't tell me they're working people.'

'They work for their living,' said Eliza firmly.

'Still they're not working people like us.'

'Annie Kenney is,' said Dora impatiently. 'And she's recruiting more working people into the WSPU. Or haven't you noticed? The WSPU is for *all* women now. That other lot, it's all, "Oh please give us the vote. You don't mind, do you? We only want to vote,"' Dora mimicked a posh voice.

29

'But where's it got them? Women still haven't got the right to vote. And it's a human right. That's what our Labour candidate, Mr Williams, wrote in the newspaper. It's a *human* right.'

'Dora,' her father said. 'That's enough now, lass.'

Dora subsided. But inside her mind was seething. It is a human right, she thought. Women should be able to have a say about what was done in their name.

'Evie – you'll make sure the bairns are put to bed, then,' said her mother, rising from her chair.

'Don't you want to come, Evie?' said Dora. She felt a bit guilty that her sister was being left behind to mind the children.

Evie laughed. 'I'd rather stop here.'

'I do what I do for you too, you know that, don't you?' Dora said.

'Aye I do. We all pull together in this family, don't we? Each in our own way.'

'We'd best get that banner ready,' said Dora's father, rising too. He put a hand on George's shoulder. 'Come on, George lad.'

'Come on, one and all,' put in Dora. 'No time to lose.' Seizing her shawl she danced ahead of the others to the doorway.

'Hold that banner aloft,' Eliza commanded. 'Let it be seen.

Let its message spread!' Her breath wound upwards in the frosty air.

'Up with it then, George lad,' said Dora's father. The two men hoisted up the banner.

Theirs wasn't the only banner on display outside the polling station, but it was the biggest and the finest, thought Dora proudly.

She shivered. It was cold, but she didn't want to go home, not yet. She wanted to stay there, drink in the excitement she felt all around her.

Her mother walked in front of the banner and surveyed it critically. 'You can't see the words,' she said. 'Move it along a bit, Jim, where it's light. And there's Mr Sherwell's lot, handing out pamphlets,' she added, nodding her head to where a group of well-dressed men and women stood talking. 'I'd like them to see it.' The two men lifted up the banner again, shuffling along with an apology here, a 'mind yourself' there.

'That's better,' Eliza said. She considered. 'Dora, go and fetch one of those pamphlets. I'd like to see what lies the man's spreading.'

As Dora darted off, her father watched, a smile on his face. Dora was a chip off the old block. She was so bright, so quick. She had a will too. Once she'd set off on a path there was no stopping young Dora.

Flo was hopping from foot to foot and blowing on her

fingers to warm them. 'Can we go home soon, Mam?' she complained. 'It's cold out here.'

'A little discomfort now is better than a lot later,' said her mother tartly.

Dora ran up to them. 'Here you are, Mam, Father,' she panted. 'Listen to this!' She held the piece of paper aloft. 'Men of Huddersfield,' she read. 'Don't be misled by socialists, suffragettes and the Tories. Vote for Sherwell.'

'The cheek o' the man!' exclaimed her mother. 'Well, no matter, we'll see how he looks after he's beaten.'

Several heads turned at her words. Dora saw one of them glance upwards at their banner and smile. In the gaslight the words shone like a beacon. The woman wove her way through the little groups of people towards them. Dora gulped, as she reached them. It was Annie Kenney whom she'd marched behind in the procession, the day the suffragettes had arrived in Huddersfield. She looked tired, Dora thought, deep shadows under her eyes. And no wonder. She'd been in prison for weeks and now was running about all over the district, gathering support for the cause.

'That's a fine banner you have there, Mrs Thewlis,' Annie said.

'Thank you, Miss Kenney,' Eliza answered. She took the hand Annie extended to her. 'We've been doing our bit to keep the Liberal out – and get the cause noticed at the same time.' She nodded at Dora. 'This is my daughter, Dora. She's been helping me.'

'I remember. We marched together, the day I arrived in Huddersfield,' laughed Annie. 'It's been a fine campaign, Mrs Thewlis. You heard what Mrs Mitchell said, didn't you? How we'll put a match to the fire you've built here in Huddersfield.'

'It's lit already. And pray God it will never go out. Come what may, the fight must go on,' said Dora's mother firmly. 'If need be more will go to prison for the cause.'

'The spirit in Huddersfield women beats anything I've met anywhere,' Annie declared. 'I've no doubt the result tonight will be what we hope for.'

Oh, please let it be! All that campaigning. Let it not be for nowt. It wouldn't be fair. It wouldn't be right. Dora looked up to see that everyone was staring at her. Had she spoken her thoughts out loud then? George was rolling his eyes, but Annie was smiling at her as if she understood.

'It's what it's all about, isn't it, Dora,' she said quietly. 'Fairness. Making things better for all people – women as well as men.'

'Oh yes,' said Dora eagerly. 'It's not just about getting the vote, it's about what is done with it.'

Annie nodded. 'That's why I joined the WSPU. I used to work in a mill,' she said. 'One day, I heard Christabel Pankhurst speak at Oldham. I never forgot what she said.

And when I found I could be of use to the cause, I walked away from the mill – and I've never looked back since.' She laughed. 'Christabel and I went to prison – in Manchester. My family only learned where I was when they read about it in the paper. They tried to pay my fine, but I wouldn't let them. Prison, or the vote. That's how I see it.' Her eyes lit up.

'After I'd been campaigning for the WSPU in the north,' Annie went on, 'the Pankhursts asked me to join them in London where they had set up office. I had little over a pound in my pocket after I had paid my train fare and all I owned was packed into one basket. I didn't know what to expect. I'd no learning. I'd never even been so far south before. Soon after I arrived in London, Sylvia Pankhurst took me to a meeting of East End women,' Annie continued. 'I told them that their lives would be better once we women got the vote. I tried to give them hope. I think I did.'

She was silent. It really matters to her, thought Dora. She really cares.

Annie sighed. 'It seems a long time ago now,' she said. 'But,' she looked earnestly at Dora. 'I've not given up hope. I've learnt that change comes – but slowly. Experience teaches you that, Dora.'

'Miss Kenney!' A woman hurried up to them. She bent to whisper in Annie's ear. Annie nodded, then turned back to the family. 'I must go,' she said. 'It seems they need help over at the Liberals' committee rooms.' She gave them a big smile. 'We're asking all the electors not to vote for him. And he doesn't like it!'

She's a fine woman, that Annie Kenney,' said Dora's mother as the women hurried away. Dora nodded slowly. She was. And she – a mill girl once like Dora – had taken charge of her life. If she could do it, so could she, Dora. One day … maybe…

Chapter Seven

'Dora! Dora! Get up, layabed. It's past six.' Evie's voice buzzed urgently in Dora's ear. She gave her sister a shake. Dora rolled over in bed and pulled the sheet up over her head. She felt as if she'd only just dropped off. Was it really time to get up? She pulled down the sheet and opened her eyes. It was still dark outside. A lit candle glowed by the bed. Evie stood next to it, already dressed. Dora rubbed her eyes. Something felt wrong. What was it? Of course, the election. It was over – and in spite of all their efforts they'd failed to dislodge the Liberal. The government would be rejoicing this morning! The women had got the cause noticed all right. But what difference had it made? There was a new Liberal MP in Parliament this morning and women were no nearer getting the vote than they had been.

Evie gave her sister another shove. 'Well, you can't say I've not warned you. That buzzer will be off any minute now and I'm not waiting any longer.'

Why must I go to the mill? Dora thought rebelliously as her sister hurried away. Why cannot I walk away, like

Annie? 'Because you're only sixteen,' a little voice said inside her head. 'You cannot leave. You must do what is expected of you.'

A bustling clatter rose up from downstairs. A door slammed. They were leaving – without her! Hurriedly, Dora dragged on her clothes and made her way down the stairs, rubbing the sleep out of her eyes.

Her father had waited for her. 'You're late. We must hurry.' He sounded put out.

Mam sounded as cross as Dad. 'Come on now, Dora,' she said impatiently. 'Don't stand there dithering. You'll make your father late. And I've a deal to do today, without worrying about that too. There's the house to put to rights, and I'm behind with the ironing.' She thrust a hunk of bread and dripping into Dora's hands. 'You'd best eat this on the way. And here – take this egg for your breakfast. It's a cold day. Mabel will be along with your dinner later.' Why was everyone so grumpy, Dora thought. It wasn't her fault they'd lost the by-election, was it? The door banged behind them.

Dora shivered as she stepped outside. Fog had wrapped itself round the town like a thick grey blanket. The sound of distant voices and the clatter – was it clogs, or a horse's hoofs? – drifted to them through the murk. Her father took her arm to guide her. It was hard to see anything at all. You had to watch your step. They crossed the road.

Beyond the rows of little terraced houses the slender mill chimneys struggled to poke their way through the fog. Everything was just as it had always been, as if the high hopes of yesterday had been merely a dream. Was it really only yesterday? How excitedly they'd talked as they'd made this same walk. The whole mill had been buzzing with expectation. And now, well, it was all over.

'Dora lass.' Reluctantly Dora raised her eyes to see that her father was looking at her. 'The world isn't ending. Our time will come. You're young ... very young ...'

Dora was silent.

'I understand how you feel,' her father said. 'I'm as disappointed as you that the Labour chap didn't get in. You take it harder when you're young. But when you're older –'

'Fifty years, Father!' Dora burst out. 'Nearly fifty years women have been fighting for the right to vote. I don't want to take it less hard.'

Her father sighed, at a loss to know what to say. He squeezed her arm. 'I know, Dora. None of it makes any sense,' he said at last. 'But remember – nothing worthwhile was ever won in a day. And have you forgotten,' he went on hurriedly as Dora looked ready to object, 'that now we have a wonderful organization working for us – the WSPU. Working for us, Dora – for you, for your mother and sisters.'

'But …' Dora began.

'Give it time, Dora lass. That's all I'm saying.'

How much time? Dora thought rebelliously. Women had been fighting for the vote ever since she could remember. Her mother had gone on about it since she was barely able to toddle. The suffragettes had even gone to prison to get the cause noticed. And they had! They had! But if they couldn't get MPs sympathetic to the cause elected to Parliament – how would they ever get the vote?

An early train rattled past. When it had gone, Dora heard the sound she heard morning and night – that of a hundred mill buzzers. In just a few minutes more the factory gates would shut and they'd be shut out too. And a day's work lost meant a day's wage lost. Her father lifted his hand and waved. 'I'll see you tonight then, Dora.' Dora waved at her father's back as he disappeared into the fog. Dora's father was a weaver, too, but he worked in a mill that specialized in fancy patterned clothes, like waistcoats. It was highly skilled work. Dora was proud of her father's skill.

The fog was lifting and now Dora could see the blackened walls of the mill. She joined the stragglers hurrying to the gate, slipping through it just before it shut. Across the yard now. Her hand still clasped the egg and the hunk of bread and dripping. She'd get one of the bobbin winders to cook the egg in the steamer for her later. She took a mouthful of bread. She could have done with a bit of tea to warm her up. The familiar mill stink hit her as she entered the weaving shed, but she had grown used to it now, and it scarcely bothered her. She hung up her shawl on a peg, rolled up her sleeves, put her hand to her hair to make sure that it was safely pinned up, then made her way carefully along the rows of looms to her place. There was barely room to shuffle between them and the floor was slippery with oil. How many years was it since she'd first walked into the weaving shed? Three? Dora counted. No, it was more than that. Be four years come next May. Longer still if you counted back the years till the day she'd begun, a half-timer, standing behind the loom, assisting the weaver. She'd been – what? – ten then? Half the day at the mill, the other half at school.

The tuner came up to her. 'Well now, Dora lass. Ready to start?' he asked cheerily. 'Never seen so many long faces as I have here this morning,' he went on. Dora forced herself to smile. 'That's more like it,' Arthur said. Big Arthur was all right, Dora thought. They were lucky. Some tuners were right beggars, didn't tune the loom right. And if it wasn't tuned right, it wouldn't run smoothly and you'd get all sorts of problems – breakages in the threads, the woven fabric snarled up. And who was it got hauled up by the menders when a piece of cloth was spoilt? Yours truly.

Arthur moved on to the loom of the girl next to her.

There was a new girl at Edie's loom this morning. Edie had got hit by a flying shuttle and hadn't been back to work since.

When Arthur had finished, the new girl glanced over at Dora.

'Hello, I'm Mary,' she said.

'And I'm Dora,' Dora smiled. 'Give us a shout if you need any help,' she added.

'Thank you,' the girl said.

There was something vaguely familiar about the girl's face, Dora thought. She wrinkled up her forehead. Where had she seen her before? If only she could remember...

Chapter Eight

'What brings you here, Mary?' said Dora. The looms had been stopped for the weavers to have their breakfast and the two girls were sitting side by side on a wall, legs swinging. For once it had been easy to find somewhere to sit. The fog had lifted but it was a raw morning and not many had come out to sit in the yard. 'Oh, that's easy,' said Mary. 'The pay's better here. Needed it really. My eldest sister's sick and Mam's got her hands full looking after her and the little 'un.'

She'd not mentioned a father, Dora noticed, cradling her hot egg in her hands. Was Mary the only breadwinner in the family? One weaver's wage was not a lot to keep a family on.

'He seems all right – Arthur,' said Mary conversationally.

'Oh aye, Big Arthur's all right,' Dora smiled. 'Just make sure to smile at him, keep your eyes on your work and you'll stay on the right side of him.'

'The tuner at my last job was a right surly so and so,' Mary said. 'Didn't matter whether you smiled at him or not. He had it in for me, and wasn't bothered whether my looms were tuned right or not. I used to dread it when the menders came in about a faulty piece.'

'Dora nodded. She was feeling more and more sure that she had seen Mary before. If only she could remember where. If only she could put that election result behind her. Absently she began to peel the egg.

'Penny for them?'

Startled, Dora looked up. She'd clean forgotten that Mary was sitting next to her. 'Sorry, Mary, I'm not myself today.'

'I feel a bit out o' sorts meself,' confessed Mary.

Dora felt ashamed of herself. What were her problems, compared to Mary's? A mother stuck at home with a baby and a sick child. The burdens always fell heaviest on the womenfolk, she thought bitterly.

'I'm sorry your sister's sick,' she ventured.

'Aye, it's a worry.' Mary hugged her knees. She hesitated. 'Everyone seems a bit gloomy here.'

'Could be the election,' Dora said, toying with the bits of eggshell in her lap. 'A lot weren't happy with the result.' She glanced sideways at Mary to see what she thought – if anything. After all, Mary had enough to worry about already. She couldn't be much older than her, Dora thought, gazing at her, but she looked as if she had had to grow up fast.

'Was a shame, wasn't it,' said Mary, with feeling. 'Such a close result. I thought we'd get the Liberal out. I really did. I tried to do my bit, got some suffragette leaflets to hand out, but then my sister took sick and Mam needed help with her and the little 'un.'

So that's where I saw her! thought Dora. At Market Cross. 'You were there, weren't you,' she exclaimed. 'At Market Cross, the night Mrs Pankhurst spoke to us. By the wagon, when we went up afterwards to offer help?' she added when Mary looked blank. 'I knew I'd seen you somewhere before.'

Mary looked startled. 'Yes, I was there,' she said. She stared hard at Dora, as if trying to remember. Then her face cleared and she laughed. 'I remember. You were there with your mother and father.'

What was it Mam had said? 'We were the first to offer Mrs Pankhurst help.' Dora smiled wryly. The look on Mary's face when Mam had said that! 'You heard Mam, didn't you?' she said. 'She gets a bit carried away at times. But her heart's in the right place. She's cared about the cause since – oh, I don't know how long. I can't remember a time when she hasn't talked about it.'

'And you?' said Mary.

Dora nodded. 'Aye, me too. Wouldn't be my mother's daughter otherwise,' she said. 'But it's not just about getting the vote, is it?' she said, seriously. 'It's what we can do with it.'

'Aye, the other lot have had their chance,' said Mary. 'The men.'

'But will our chance ever come?' said Dora disconsolately. 'Now the Liberal's got in again … in spite of everything…' Her voice trailed away. She felt so weary suddenly.

'It's just one by-election, Dora,' said Mary. 'Just one. I'm disappointed too, but I'm not giving up that easily! What was it I heard the suffragettes said afterwards: "We have given the government such a fighting as they have never had before." She laughed. 'And it's true. It's not over, Dora. It's just beginning.'

Dora felt her spirits lift. If Mary could stay hopeful in spite of all her problems, so could she.

'Thanks, Mary,' she said.

'What for?' asked Mary.

'Making me feel better,' Dora smiled. 'Come on, let's get back. It's too cold to sit out here.'

The two girls stood up.

'We'll talk again, shall we?' Dora asked hopefully.

Mary nodded her head vigorously. 'We will.' She smiled. 'Seems that we have a lot to talk about!'

'You'll be back tomorrow, then?' Dora said to Mary as the looms came to a stop. 'Not running off to get a new job,' she joked. Mary pulled a face. She knew as well as Dora that weavers had a bit of a reputation for ducking out of a job if a better one beckoned. But who could blame them, Dora thought. If the pay was better, if weaving wasn't such an awful job, maybe they'd stay put in one place longer. No one liked the weaving shed. The heat. The endless noise, the toil. No one who had the choice hung about there. The bobbin winders nipped in and out as fast as they could. The beamer who set up a new piece for the weavers, the numberers who pulled a face every time they came in to tick someone off, hands over their ears … awful fuss *they* made.

'I'll be back,' Mary said, unhooking her shawl and pulling it over her head.

Leaving the mill behind them, the two girls walked down the road, turning south towards the town. A brisk wind had brought down the last of the autumn leaves. The sun had long ago sunk, a fiery red, behind the hills. It would be a cold day again tomorrow.

'I turn off here,' said Dora, as they reached the road that ran under the railway viaduct. 'Home's only about another five minutes' walk away. Which way are you going?'

Mary jerked her head to the left. 'Into town. I live round Castlegate.'

Dora stared. 'That's a fair way,' she stammered trying to hide her surprise. Castlegate! Only those who had no choice lived in one of the streets and yards round Castlegate. Some people reckoned it was one step up from the workhouse.

'Aye,' said Mary, casually, as if it was of no account. 'My last workplace was nearer home, but it wasn't half as nice a place as this.'

Must have been pretty bad then, Dora thought. Poor Mary. How did she manage to keep so cheerful?

Mary raised her hand. 'See you in the morning.'

'See you in the morning,' Dora echoed. It was a bit of a trudge into Castlegate, Dora knew. And she doubted Mary'd have money to spare for the tram ride. She ran across the road, as a train rattled by overhead. As she walked up to Hawthorne Terrace she saw – as if seeing it for the first time – how neat it was. The two rows of terraced houses facing each other, small but tidy gardens in front. The long flagstoned path that ran between them. Old houses maybe, no gas lighting in them like some had, and you heard every train that rumbled by, but palaces compared to the dwellings in the streets round Castlegate. Dora shuddered. When all was said and done, she was luckier than many.

Chapter Nine

'Where's Mam?' asked Dora, opening the door to no. 29.

Her father was shovelling coals on to the fire. He stood up, wiping his hands. 'She's round at Mrs Key's. You remember Mrs Key,' he said. 'She was down at Market Cross, the day Mrs Pankhurst spoke there.' He smiled and whispered in Dora's ear as if it was a great secret. 'Your mam's learnt that Mrs Pankhurst is coming back to Huddersfield next week. There's to be a big meeting. And your mam thinks it's because of the interest roused in the WSPU since the by-election.' He tapped his nose. 'Don't say I told you though. Let it be a surprise.'

'Oh, Dad!' exclaimed Dora. 'Isn't that grand?'

'Your mam's been running round Huddersfield rustling up support,' her father went on. 'Seems she's met a lot who feel like us about votes for women. And some live right on our doorstep.' He laughed. 'She'll have them round here soon enough, see if I'm not right.'

Dora slid into a chair and took off her clogs to rub her tired feet. She'd have flat feet by the time she was twenty, all that standing, day in day out. She'd hardly seen her mam over the past few days. So that was why! The Pankhursts were coming back to Huddersfield. To Dora's mind it could mean only one thing. The WSPU were going to set up a new branch, right here in Huddersfield, if they could get enough keen to join. And if anyone could, her mam could!

It was only a couple of days later that Dora discovered that her father was right. Opening the door one evening she found herself face to face with a load of women.

'Come on in, Dora,' her mother boomed. 'Don't hang about on that doorknob. You look like a startled hen.' Dora blinked, one hand still on the door. Was she dreaming? Who were all these people?

Her mother smiled. 'Welcome,' she said, nodding her head at the assembled women, 'to the Huddersfield branch of the WSPU!'

'Now, Mrs Thewlis, that is a little premature,' a woman's voice broke in mildly.

Mrs Thewlis ignored the interruption. 'This is my daughter, Dora,' she said to the women who crowded the front room. Every chair was occupied, Dora saw, every bit of space was filled, women propped up the range and leant back against the chimneypiece, and the rest were squashed together on the bottom stairs and the floor.

Dora felt as if her head was spinning. Mam had been busy, all right.

'Yes indeed,' said a woman eagerly from the huddle round the range – a neighbour who had moved in to the terrace not long ago. 'Your mother told me how you and she spearheaded the recent by-election campaign in Huddersfield.' Dora saw some of the women exchange glances, as if to say that was news to them.

'Don't look so surprised, lass,' laughed her mother as a woman shifted up obligingly to make room for her. 'We're just meeting to get things going. Mrs Pankhurst and her daughter Miss Adela Pankhurst – the WSPU's regional organizer for the north country,' she explained – 'are coming up to Huddersfield to set up a new branch of the WSPU.' She paused and surveyed her audience. All eyes were upturned to her. Mam knew how to hold a crowd, Dora thought, it was just one of her many gifts.

'We've all heard the rumours, but that's all it is – rumours,' said a voice from somewhere near the staircase.

'Yes, we can't be sure why they're coming,' someone put in from another corner of the room.

Eliza turned to the doubters. 'We can,' she said firmly. 'What other reason could there be? Don't let folk tell you otherwise. Mrs Pankhurst personally thanked me for the hard work put in by the women of Huddersfield in the recent campaign. And she said that she'd seen nowt like it, in any other place. And,' she carried on, scarcely stopping to draw breath, 'Mrs Hannah Mitchell said it was like we'd

put a torch to a fire. We must make sure it doesn't go out –
not until we women have got what we deserve – the vote.'

'Well said, lass,' said a male voice, over by the door.
Dora looked up to see that her father had come quietly in.
It was as her dad had expected, Dora thought – though not
maybe such numbers. But if he was surprised to see such
an array of women in his home he didn't show it. He took
off his cap and nodded to the assembled women.

'There'll be a role for our menfolk,' said Eliza, smiling
at him. 'We all know that not everyone in this town agrees
that we women should have the vote, we're used to the
heckles and jeers of the ignorant. But my husband Jim' –
Dora's father bowed – 'has always been a stalwart supporter
of the cause and he – and I'm sure others of our menfolk
– will make sure we don't have any trouble.'

'This is all very fine, Mrs Thewlis,' one of the women
put in gently. 'But do we have a date when we may expect
the Pankhursts?'

'Aye, 'ave we got a date?' said another woman.

Dora's mother looked round the assembled women. 'We
have. Next Tuesday. The Town Hall has been booked.' Dora
saw the women look at each other. 'We'll need to advertise
the meeting, of course. It's important that there's a good
turn-out. I and my daughter Dora will of course do our bit.
We hope some of you'll be able to offer help, too.

'But now,' she said briskly, 'seeing as we're all good

socialist women here, we'll have a quick sing and then a cup of tea. Dora, you'll put the kettle on.'

There was nothing that the socialist women of Huddersfield liked more than a right good sing – and a cup of tea, Dora thought as she ran into the scullery to fill the kettle. The words of 'the Red Flag' resounded round the room. So Mrs Pankhurst was returning to Huddersfield – to set up a new branch of the WSPU. Mary had been right. Dora found herself smiling as she lifted down cups and saucers from the dresser. It wasn't all over. It was just beginning.

Chapter Ten

'You should have heard us, Mary,' Dora said. 'Surprised the neighbours didn't bang on the walls!' She grinned. 'Mam must have been right round the neighbourhood rounding up everyone she'd heard was sympathetic to the cause. I never knew our house could fit in so many.'

Mary laughed. 'It sounds grand.'

'Oh, and I've something to show you!' Dora said. She held out a length of calico. Mary peered at it. The words 'VOTES FOR WOMEN' were inscribed on it. 'I made it last night,' Dora said proudly. 'It's a sash.'

'It's beautiful,' said Mary admiringly. 'When will you wear it?'

'Tonight, when I stand out in the street, drumming up support for the meeting. We want to get as many along as we can,' Dora said. 'Don't want the Pankhursts to speak to an empty hall. They might change their minds about setting up the branch.' She laughed. 'You know, I half thought Mam was jesting at first – she does get a bit carried away at times – but she's right. Mrs Pankhurst is coming to Huddersfield. She's going to speak at the Town Hall on Tuesday.'

'And you're certain that's why they're coming?' said Mary.

'Like Mam said, I can't think why else,' said Dora. 'Do come, Mary. It'll be a grand do.' Dora knew that Mary was as fired up by the cause as she was. And she liked her, admired the way she made the best of things.

'I'll 'ave to see,' said Mary. 'If only there were more than 24 hours in a day.' She tilted her head back and stared up at the sky. Somewhere a rook cawed. The two girls watched its progress across the grey winter sky, a black dot winging its way over the rooftops and mill chimneys, over and away into the hills. It had snowed in the night. The snow had soon turned to a muddy slush in the town, but a fair scattering of white still lay on the hills. 'You're lucky to have time to go to meetings.'

I am, thought Dora, folding up the sash carefully. Whenever she felt discontented she reminded herself how much easier life was for her than for Mary – and for so many others. She'd been in parts of town where the truly poor lived, those who had lost their jobs, or who were too old or sick to work, seen the grimy back-to-back courts, the thin, pinched faces of scrawny children running about the streets barefoot and in rags, and it hurt her, it did, but somehow it was only when someone you knew was affected that it truly hit home how much was wrong in the country. Mary had confided that her father had died. Typhoid fever, she'd said. Her mam had blamed the bad drains. But at least they managed to scrape a living, Mary said, and to stay together. They hadn't had to go to the workhouse.

Dora looked into her friend's face. She could swear that it had grown thinner. She wondered how bad things really were at home.

'Looks like it will snow again,' said Mary. It did, thought Dora, staring up at the sky and grimacing. It looked as if a bucketful of the stuff was about to empty on them.

'What will you do if it snows tonight?' said Mary.

'I'll still go,' said Dora. 'I promised Mam I would. I'll be all right. Mam'll be campaigning alongside me.'

It was an important job she had to do tonight but, Dora sighed, one that meant getting covered with snow by the look of things.

'Votes for women,' Dora bawled. Her voice was growing hoarse. Could anyone actually hear her? she wondered. Maybe here, near the Exchange, wasn't the best place to advertise a suffragette meeting. And on an evening like this too. A few people had stopped out of curiosity and she'd grinned and told them about the meeting that was being held on Tuesday night at the Town Hall. Some of them shook their heads at her disapprovingly. What did she think she was doing, a girl handing out leaflets on the street? But others had shaken her warmly by the hand and said they'd be there. Plenty more sailed right past, businessmen on their way home from the Exchange, well wrapped up in warm winter coats against the chill. She giggled. She didn't expect them to stop and listen! Some women arm in arm with their husbands looked as if they wanted to stop and talk to her but didn't dare. But maybe, thought Dora, they'd find a way to sneak along to the meeting. Plenty of well-to-do women had joined the WSPU.

She stamped her feet. They felt like ice inside her boots. How long had she been standing there? Since six – and it must be long past that now. Mam had left her to go down to the station. Dora wished that she had gone with her. You got a lot of people through there. Before she'd gone, she'd warned Dora to keep off the pavement. You could be hauled up by the police for obstructing a pathway.

How many would come to the meeting? Dora wondered. Would the hall be as packed as it had been last month? The election was behind them now, and people had other things on their minds a week before Christmas – like how they'd pay for the turkey and Christmas presents.

It had begun to snow again. Snowflakes whirled in the gaslight, thick and fast. Dora shivered and wrapped her arms around herself. Her shawl felt wet and heavy. She was wasting her time, hanging about here. All sensible people had long gone home. Even those young lads who always hung about had mostly run off now. She'd pack up and as soon as a tram came along she'd hop on it.

A snowball flew past her ear. 'Eh! You young rascal, what do you think you're doing?' a man shouted. Dora looked round to see a wagoner brush snow off his shoulders. He shook his fist at a boy who scampered off. Dora gave a wry smile. He'd caught the snowball meant for her. Young lads, they were the worst. No respect.

She reached the stop just as a tram rounded the corner. There were only a couple of people ahead of her, women with baskets looped over their arms. The women looked at her curiously as they climbed on. Had they heard her, seen her sash? Dora wondered, as she slid into a seat near the front.

The tram drove slowly through the town, stopping occasionally to let people on board. The floor ran wet with melted snow, but at least inside it was warm. The newer trams had electric heaters – a far cry from the old days shivering on the open upper deck. Dora closed her eyes. Her eyelids felt so heavy, too heavy to keep open.

The sharp end of an umbrella jabbing into her side jerked Dora awake. She opened her eyes to see that the tram had come to a stop again.

Next to her a large woman laden with shopping was struggling to her feet. 'Where are we?' Dora asked sleepily.

'Bradford Road, lass,' the woman answered.

It was her stop! Dora leapt to her feet and hurried along

the corridor, jumping off the tram just in time. The tram sailed on into the dark. Dora trudged across the road. It was quiet, as if the little terraced houses had all settled down to sleep under their cosy blankets of snow. And just as soon as she got inside, Dora thought with a sleepy yawn, that was what she was going to do, too.

Chapter Eleven

The hall was around three-quarters full – a good number
for a meeting held so close to Christmas, Dora thought,
slipping into the seat Mam had kept for her near the front.
She'd spent the last half-hour handing out leaflets at the
entrance, staying until she saw the cab bearing the speakers
draw up. As it had got near the hall a woman had peered
out, her face breaking into a smile when she saw Dora.

'Votes for women,' Annie Kenney called. 'Yours in the
cause,' Dora shouted back. From inside the cab a sea of
hands waved at her.

Now, sitting in the hall, Dora could feel excitement
crackle all around her. There had been more suffragette
arrests. What better publicity could there be to get the new
branch of the WSPU up and running?

For Mam had been right! Mrs Pankhurst had returned
to set up a new branch. All the interest they'd roused at
the election must not be allowed to wither away, Mrs
Pankhurst told them, in ringing tones. They must build
on what had been achieved here in Huddersfield. Some
criticized their tactics, she said, but they had roused the

interest of the town, and they would not abandon them. Women were in prison again and would continue to go to prison until the government gave women what they wanted – the vote! When she sat down, Dora thought the applause would lift off the roof.

She glanced across at her mother. Eliza was smiling broadly. A few rows behind them sat Mrs Key and her husband and a group of women, heads close, talking. If only Mary was here…

'Who will volunteer to join the new branch?' she heard a voice call suddenly from the platform.

The moment had come! People began to rise to their feet, in ones and twos, some looking round to see what their friends and neighbours were doing. 'Come along, Dora,' her mother said, 'you heard them. We're off to sign up.' Mrs Key was up on her feet too now, and her mam pointed out Miss Beever who lived over in Crosland Moor and Mrs Pinnance who lived in the Paddock area. There were others too, whose faces looked familiar. Some of them had been at 29 Hawthorne Terrace the day her mam announced that the Pankhursts were returning to Huddersfield, Dora recalled. They made their way along the row to the platform, waiting their turn to sign up. An awful lot more though were shuffling towards the exit, or hadn't moved from their seats. How could they sit there so calmly? Dora wondered. Hadn't they been moved like her by Annie Kenney's words? When women got the vote, she had told them, they could say goodbye to seeing children starve on the street, to the despair of men and women who had no work, the old who had no home to go to but the workhouse.

'Join us,' she had urged. 'Young women of Huddersfield, join us. And make the lives of your mothers easier and happier.' It was almost, Dora felt, as if Annie was appealing to her personally.

As soon as the meeting was over, Eliza took charge. 'The first thing we must do is call everyone together,' she said as they stood with the others who'd signed up in a huddle outside the hall.

'Mrs Thewlis, Mrs Pankhurst says that she will arrange a meeting for those who've put their names forward tonight,' said a quiet voice, 'when she will explain the objects of the movement and its constitution.'

'Aye, of course, Mrs Key,' Eliza said. 'There may be some who need guidance on that.'

Dora caught one or two of the women exchanging glances as if to say, that Mrs Thewlis, she'll take over if we give her an inch. Well, and so what if she does, thought Dora. They were lucky to have her. She'd rarely heard a better speaker than her mam and you'd go far to find a worker more committed to the cause.

'You're late back.' Jim raised his eyes questioningly as Dora and her mother let themselves into the house. 'How'd it go?' Dora took off her coat and hat and slung her damp coat over the clothes horse in front of the range to dry. A huge smile spread over her face.

'It's welcome to the newest branch of the WSPU,' said Eliza jubilantly, as she unpinned her hat.

Jim got up and shook both their hands in turn. 'It's the best news,' he said, smiling broadly. 'And who's running it?' he said, winking at Dora.

Her mother didn't see the wink. 'Well, we'll see about that. It's not been decided yet.'

Jim settled back in his chair and lit his pipe. 'I want to hear all about it. So,' he said looking expectantly up at them. 'Who's going to be first?'

Chapter Twelve

'I wish you had been there, Mary,' Dora said to her friend. Mary looked tired, Dora thought. No, more than tired – as if she had not slept at all.

It was the morning after the meeting. All morning Dora had been bursting to tell Mary about it. After the meeting had ended a group of them had piled into the kitchen of one of the new members, who lived not far from Hawthorne Terrace. They'd talked and laughed and made plans till the fire in the grate had dwindled into glowing embers. Already there was much to discuss.

The Pankhursts would return to the town in the new year to set up the branch, and then when the branch was up and running there'd be a new campaign to think about. There were all sorts of rumours flying about what that might be, the biggest that there was to be a great march on the House of Commons the day after the King's Speech in February. Would anyone from the fledgling branch take part? Dora's head had buzzed excitedly, while her hands moved automatically across the piece of fabric on the loom in front of her, watching for loose threads, deftly tying them up. The noise hardly bothered her at all this morning.

'I'm sorry, Dora, I'm not myself today.' Dora looked up at Mary. Her face looked miserable. Dora felt ashamed of herself for gabbling on. Mary had been in trouble for making a mistake earlier that morning and in all her jubilation about the new branch Dora had quite forgotten. How could she be so thoughtless?

She put out a hand and lightly touched her friend's arm. 'Don't let it worry you,' she said. 'We all make mistakes. You're a good weaver.'

All the weavers dreaded it when the numberers came down from the mending department to see a weaver about a fault in a piece. Each piece was numbered, as were the looms, so the numberers knew at once who was responsible for the fault. Mary had had to go up to the mending department to explain herself. Poor Mary. Was it any wonder that her concentration had lapsed for a moment, Dora thought. She had too much on her mind these days.

Mary shook her head. 'It's not that,' she said. She paused and said in a low voice, 'We're moving.'

'Moving!' exclaimed Dora. 'You're not leaving Huddersfield, are you?'

Mary shook her head. 'No, we're not moving away, we're going to live at my uncle's.' She swallowed. 'We couldn't really manage – not on what Mam brought in and my wage – but my uncle earns good money. It'll be easier...' Her voice trailed off. Her fingers were tightly clasped in her lap.

So why did she look so unhappy?

'Thing is,' said Mary, 'I don't like him. He lords it over us, and my aunt is not much better – they treat us like servants.'

Dora didn't know what to say. She laid her hand on her friend's and pressed it. 'Maybe it will be better than you think,' she said at last. 'Where will you be living?'

'Near Hillhouse Lane.'

'Why, that's near us!' exclaimed Dora. 'We'll be practically neighbours.' Hillhouse Lane was also a step from the slaughterhouse and cattle market. On windy days you could smell it. But it was a whole lot better than down by Castlegate.

Mary nodded. 'I'm glad about that,' she said.

'We'll find a way,' Dora said cheerily. She felt sorry for Mary, but nothing could entirely dampen her good spirits today.

They'd started something in Huddersfield, she thought as she walked home that evening. They'd lit a match. Soon the whole of the north would be alight. And then ... let them at Parliament look out!

Chapter Thirteen

A blast of steam hit Dora as she opened the door of 29 Hawthorne Terrace. It was Monday – washday – and the house was full of damp washing. Damp woollen shawls were draped over the clothes horse next to newly washed clothes. Dora wrinkled up her nose. They smelt horrible.

'You've taken your time, the others have been back these thirty minutes at least,' her mother said, bustling into the kitchen. Her face looked red and hot.

'Sorry, Mam,' said Dora contritely.

Her mother pushed a strand of damp hair back off her face. 'Well, now you're here you can make yourself useful. Give Evie a hand with that mangle. She can't turn it on her own. And I've the bairns to see to. Arthur's got a cold and been under me feet all day driving me distracted.'

Dora went into the scullery and took hold of one arm of the mangle. The last batch of wet clothes was being wrung out one more time.

'Fold 'em up and we'll dry them in the morning,' said her mother, putting her head round the door. Just doing that took an age. Mam was really particular. Everything had to be folded and hung out carefully to make the clothes and sheets easier to iron. 'I may have other things on me mind right now, but I'll not have anyone say I can't keep the house nice,' Eliza said.

'Where's Flo?' asked Dora, as – wet clothes in a neat pile – they went outside to hang up the tin baths that they had used to rinse the washing.

'Gone out to buy tea. Mam forgot it earlier. She's all in a fluster.'

'She allus is on washday,' said Dora.

'It'll get worse once the branch is properly up and running,' said Evie.

'She'll have them all hopping about,' said Dora.

Evie laughed. '*You'll* 'ave them hopping about – you and Mam both.' The branch had better look out, she thought. Mam and Dora meant business.

Dora followed Evie back into the kitchen, arms full of damp clothes. Women's work never ended, she thought wearily. And many had to work too, and had children to care for. Damp was running down the inside of the windows. The house was like a laundry on washday. And when it wasn't the washing, it was the ironing. When it wasn't ironing, it was cleaning.

Thursday was fettling day – the day when every house was cleaned from the stone steps out front to the panes of glass in the windows. But nothing could keep the dirt out

67

for long in a mill town like Huddersfield. It crept in from the railway and the mill chimneys and the house had to have a once-over every day.

Friday was bake day. Dora loved coming home to the smell of freshly baked bread, pay in her pocket too. Most of it went into the family purse, of course.

Dora's father had come in while the girls were out the back, and had settled himself down in his chair, his copy of *The Worker* on his knee. He lit his pipe. Dora looked at her father enviously. However hard men worked it was harder for women. How often did she get time to read? And soon she'd have even less.

Flo put her head round the door. 'I've got the tea, Mam,' she called. She put the packet of tea down on the table, and rubbed her hands together. 'Brrr, but it's cold out there,' she said. 'Where's Mam? I got a message for her.'

Dora jerked her head towards the staircase. Squeals of laughter drifted down. 'Up with the bairns.'

'Well, it don't matter – I can tell you instead.' She grinned at Dora. 'Since it concerns you too. It's from Mrs Key. She was in the queue ahead of me at the shop. The Pankhursts are coming back to Huddersfield. There's to be a meeting of all those who've signed up to join the WSPU, next week in Robinson's Cafe!'

Chapter Fourteen

'So how did it go?' asked Mary. 'The meeting, yesterday?'

'We were quite a crowd,' Dora said. She hugged her knees. 'Don't think the manager of the cafe knew what had hit him! There was Mrs Pankhurst and Mrs Martel. Adela Pankhurst was there too – she's our regional organizer. She'll tell us how to go about things. And,' Dora laughed, 'Mrs Pankhurst said that seeing as how we're outlaws from society we're justified in behaving like outlaws – making raids on Parliament and suchlike, until they give in and give us the vote.'

It was more or less what Mam had said to that woman when they'd been managing the table during the by-election campaign, Dora recalled suddenly. How long ago that seemed. 'Should have seen his face when Mrs Pankhurst said that!' Her eyes sparkled mischievously.

'Who are the members then? Do they all live in Huddersfield?' Mary asked.

Dora shook her head. 'No, a lot live outside the town. We're going over to Berry Brow soon. Mary Gawthorpe's speaking at the Labour Club and Mam's to chair the meeting!' she said proudly. 'We're bound to pull in a fair number. Miss Gawthorpe's a good speaker, and very popular. She's going to explain why the suffragettes are just fighting for women's right to vote.' It was a tricky one. Not all men had the vote and the idea that a woman should have the vote was still about as far-fetched to most people as a woman landing on the moon. She sounded so bold and confident, Mary thought, gazing at her friend. She had really settled down amongst these people, taken like a duck to water to the new life that beckoned.

Dora fished in her pocket. 'I have something to show you – my membership card. Look.' She held out the card to Mary.

'It's lovely,' said Mary, gazing at it. On one side there was a picture of women, wearing the shawl and clogs of the mill girl. 'Could almost be us, couldn't it, ' she said smiling wryly.

'Sylvia Pankhurst designed it,' said Dora. 'She's an artist. And there are postcards too – of the WSPU's leaders.'

'One day maybe you'll be on one of them postcards,' said Mary.

'Give over!' said Dora. 'Oh!' She clapped her hand to her forehead. 'I nearly forgot. I got you something.' She pulled out a little round object from her pocket and handed it to Mary. 'It's a button badge,' she explained.

Mary turned it over in her hand. 'Votes for women,'

she said slowly, reading the words written on it. 'Thank you, Dora,' she said simply. 'I'll treasure it.' She slipped the badge into her pocket.

'Will you wear it?' Dora asked eagerly.

'I will, but not at home, in case my uncle finds out. He's been going on about the suffragettes ever since he heard about the new branch. Don't know how he found out, but the fuss he makes about it. He says he won't allow a suffragette through his door. To hear him talk you'd think the country would go to ruin if women got the vote. An' me aunt's not much better.'

'But you are one of us still, aren't you?' said Dora.

'In spirit anyway,' said Mary. 'An' when I'm eighteen and able to go my own way – why then I'll be a proper suffragette, like you.' She would too, thought Dora, looking at her friend's determined face.

She leant over and gave her a hug.

'Come to a meeting then?'

'Better not. If me uncle were to find out…'

'Well, come to tea then. Meet the family.'

'I'd like that,' said Mary.

'Come next Friday,' said Dora. There'd be fresh bread straight out of the oven. Muffins and teacakes too, maybe. She'd make sure that Mary had a full stomach for once.

Mary nodded. 'Next Friday.'

'You won't forget?' said Dora.

'As if I would.'

'It's a promise then?'

'Aye, it's a promise.'

Chapter Fifteen

'Sit yourself down, Mary. Make yourself at home.' Dora's mother nodded at the spare chair at the table. Mary slid into it.

'Thank you, Mrs Thewlis,' she murmured. She felt shy suddenly, seeing so many eyes on her.

'You're very welcome,' Dora's mother replied. 'We're pleased to meet you at last. Dora's told us a lot about you.'

All Dora's sisters were there for tea, agog to hear about the new branch's progress. Even the two eldest – Mary and Amy – had dropped by. Dora was the only one of the sisters who had signed up to the new branch, but it was clear to Mary from all the eager questions that they were a close and affectionate family and proud of their young sister.

Dora hoped that the tea would be a success. The family had made a real effort, she thought proudly. The house had been given the once-over, the best china taken out and dusted for their guest. And not only freshly baked bread and jam, but ham and cakes were piled up on the table. It was a real Yorkshire tea. Just so long as Mam didn't go on too long. Usually, Dora didn't mind, but today... She glanced at Mary to see what she thought. But Mary didn't seem to mind. She was even wearing the badge she'd given her! Mam was telling them about the new committee. Dora had been very proud to learn that her mother was a member of it. Mrs Key was the very capable secretary.

'I see you're wearing one of our badges,' Dora's mother said suddenly.

Mary touched it. 'Dora gave it to me.'

Eliza smiled. 'Dora and I – we make a grand team. I don't know what we'd do without her. Eighty have signed up to the new branch now!' she said. 'We've lots of plans.

'You can do a lot with such a large membership,' said Dora eagerly.

'Just so long as they all pull their weight, Dora,' her mother reminded her. 'I have me doubts about one or two of them.' She offered Mary another slice of ham. 'I like to see a good appetite,' she said approvingly, as Mary took a piece. 'We've even pulled in one of the NUWSS's members! Miss Bertha Lowenthal,' she went on proudly.

'Very posh she is,' put in Dora.

'Aye, and she said to us that the WSPU had done more to wake up the public to the cause in twelve months than the NUWSS had managed in twelve years of petitions and letter writing,' said her mother. 'And even their leader, Mrs Fawcett, acknowledges as much…' She looked at Mary expectantly. 'Will you be joining us? We'd be pleased to have you.'

Oh, if only Mam hadn't said that. Dora squirmed and said hastily, 'Mary's awful busy. But I'm sure she'd like to – some day.'

'Let the lass speak for herself, Dora,' said her mother.

'Oh well … I would like to, Mrs Thewlis,' said Mary earnestly. 'But me mam needs me help. And my uncle is none too keen on the cause. I'm not sure what he'd say if he heard I'd signed up! But one day I hope to change his mind.'

Dora's mother laughed. They all did. 'Plenty feel like that, I'm afraid,' she said. 'They think voting is a man's business only. They'd like us to stop at home and keep our opinions to ourselves. But it's important we speak up and show them that we have our own minds – and intend to use them.'

It must have been a full hour before Eliza said she must go, she was sorry, but she had a call or two to make before it got too late.

'You must come again,' she said to Mary. 'Been a pleasure meeting you. And I hope one day we will see you at a meeting.'

Mary got up soon afterwards. 'I'd best go, they'll be wondering at home where I am,' she said. Dora went with her to the door.

'You've a grand family,' Mary said enviously as Dora opened the door. 'Close. Warm. So different from…' She shrugged. 'And your mam – I've rarely heard one talk so well.'

'I hope you didn't mind,' said Dora, 'what Mam said. Hassling you to join. The cause means a lot to her.'

'I didn't mind,' said Mary.

'So,' said Dora. 'You'll come again?'

'I will,' replied Mary, 'I've had a lovely afternoon.' She hesitated, as if there was something more she wanted to say. Then she leant forward and laid a hand on Dora's arm, 'An' I might just come to one of those meetings after all.'

Chapter Sixteen

'What are you doing this evening, Dora?' said Flo as Dora caught up with her sisters at the mill gate.

'Going home like you,' Dora said. She tucked an arm through each of her sisters'.

'Makes a change,' muttered Flo.

'Now that's not fair,' said Evie. 'Dora does her bit.' She squeezed her sister's arm affectionately. 'All the same, mind you take care, Dora,' she said seriously. Some of the hecklings the suffragettes met were turning nasty, she'd heard. She didn't want her little sister to get hurt.

'When I'm eighteen let them watch out,' declared Dora. 'There'll be no stopping me then.' She grinned at her sisters. Flo looked at her sister, suspiciously. She hoped that Dora was teasing them. Sometimes Dora didn't know when to stop.

And I'll be seventeen in a few months, Dora thought. Not long now. She longed to be part of a big campaign. The new branch was going from strength to strength. She would have liked to help canvass for new members but that was down to the properly grown-up members, which was all of them except Dora.

The girls crossed the road under the railway bridge and strolled up to Hawthorne Terrace. Hanging out of the window a few doors down from no. 29 was Mrs Brown. ''Allo, Miss Thewlis. You've 'ad a visitor. One of them suffragettes,' she called. That's right, shout it from the rooftops, Dora thought, smiling sweetly up at the window. Mrs Brown had a good heart, but she was right nosy, ear out for everyone's business. You didn't say anything in front of her that you didn't want the whole town to hear about.

But who could the visitor have been? Dora pushed down the urge to run to the door. Mrs Brown was still watching and Dora didn't want to give the old busybody something else to gossip about. But as soon as the door was shut, she ran ahead of her sisters into the kitchen.

'Father! Mam!' she cried. The kitchen was empty. Dora whirled round on her heel. Where were they? As if he'd heard her, her father came downstairs, Arthur over one shoulder.

The girls looked at each other in surprise. Their father left to mind the bairns? It wasn't a man's job. 'Where's Mam?' asked Flo.

Her father deposited Arthur on the floor with a sigh. 'Am I glad you girls are back. Your mam's gone out. In a bit of a hurry.' He turned to Dora. 'You've missed some excitement. Mrs Key's just been round to see Mam. She's had a telegram from Head Office. Seems that the Pankhurst lass and Mary Gawthorpe – they're rustlin' up support for a new campaign.'

Dora caught her breath. 'I heard we'd had a visitor,' she said. 'That old busybody Mrs Brown was full of it. So,' she said flopping into a chair and looking up at her father expectantly. 'When's it to be?'

Her father scratched his head. 'February 13th – the day after the King's Speech in Parliament. But mind you keep it under your hat for now.'

As soon as that! 'Oh, Dad!' Dora leapt up and clutched her father's arm. It wasn't hard to guess what sort of campaign it would be. Another raid on Parliament. It had to be. There was nothing in the King's Speech about any bill that would give women the vote – because there wasn't one. Yet again, the Liberal government had broken its word to the women.

But who would be brave enough to go down to London, risk being thrown in prison for the cause? Oh, if only she'd been home when Mrs Key had called. Dora walked restlessly around the room.

'So who do you think will go then, Dad?' she asked, her back to her father. Her father's eyes twinkled. 'Eh, you're jumping three steps ahead. Just you be patient. That's all I know, so it's no good trying to wheedle anything out of me. Your mam will tell you all you need to know in good time. Now while you're waiting, why don't you make us all a cup of tea? You look as if you're in need of one.'

It seemed like hours to Dora before Mam got back. 'Sit still, Dora, if you can't do anything useful, you're like a jumpin' bean,' Flo grumbled. But how could she sit still? How could she attend to anything?

Tea was cold on the table when the door opened at last to admit Eliza. Excitement wasn't just written on her face, it seemed to pour through the door with her. It had to be true.

'There's to be a new campaign, isn't there? Mrs Key's been round, hasn't she? What did she say? What's it all about?' Dora gabbled eagerly, before Eliza had even taken off her coat and hat.

'Let me catch me breath first, Dora,' said her mother. 'Yes,' she said at last. 'There's to be a big meeting – a woman's parliament, at Caxton Hall, in London. And then, if we don't get the answer we want from the government, the women will march to Parliament with their petition.' Her eyes sparkled. 'Keep it to yourselves for now though. We don't want the news leaking out to the wrong people.'

'Deeds, not words,' said Dora softly. At last! 'So who's goin' to London to represent Huddersfield then?'

'That's the big question,' her mother said, as she helped herself to tea. 'We've got to find enough willing to go to prison. It's a lot to ask. But Miss Pankhurst and Miss Gawthorpe are very persuasive.'

'But if it's for the cause, Mam, surely – ' Dora said eagerly.

Flo raised her eyes. 'Well some of us have too much to do here to go runnin' off to London. Bairns to care for, chores to do, work…'

Dora's eyes flashed. 'They're doing it for you. For us all. That's what Annie Kenney and Mary Gawthorpe say. We're helping by doing this. I in my way, you in yours,' she added, contritely.

'Girls, girls,' put in Eliza. 'Please! Don't quarrel. I don't know what I'd do without my big girls,' she smiled at Flo and Evie, 'or my young suffragette,' beaming at Dora.

It's all very well, Dora grumbled to herself, as she carried the dirty plates through into the scullery. I help in the house, tramp all around the town doing my bit for the cause – and all on top of a long day's work.

But would she have it any different? she asked herself. And the answer came in a flash. No, she wouldn't. She felt so – so *alive* – now that they were actually doing things, not just talking about it.

Chapter Seventeen

The next few days passed in a whirl. Mam was hardly ever home, the branch members were all running around trying to rustle up delegates prepared to go to London. There were tram rides out to the Colne Valley villages where many of the members lived, and secret meetings to discuss arrangements. Their hard work bore fruit. But not much. Dora was disgusted. All that effort and only four found prepared to take a stand. Four! Out of 80 signed-up members! What about the other 76?

Over in Lockwood two housekeepers, an aunt and niece – Ellen Beever and Annie Sykes – were amongst them.

Then there'd been the grand day when Adela Pankhurst had descended on the Thewlis household, the day the committee had met there. The best china was wheeled out for her. Dora ran around making cups of tea for them all. It wasn't quite the role she'd have chosen for herself, but it was something to be in the same room as Miss Pankhurst and listen to the committee members' earnest conversations.

There was plenty to discuss. Who would put up the

women for the night before the great demonstration? Then there was the train journey to London to arrange, the women's expenses. Then after the issues had been talked out, they had drifted on to politics. Oh, but it was grand. They northerners would show the rest of them what stuff they were made of. It all seemed to have happened so fast. In only a few days' time the delegates would be waved off from Huddersfield station.

'So you're not goin', Dora?' teased Mary.

'Me! No!' Dora laughed. 'I'm still only sixteen. I'd like to see their faces if I put my name forward. No one's going to give me the vote. Mam's been up and down and all over wearing out her shoe leather, trying to winkle out any willing to take part. It hasn't been easy … The menfolk', she snorted, 'can't manage without us for a few days – it's as if the world will collapse if a few women go to London for a bit. And yet they don't think fit to give women the vote!' She shrugged. 'Anyway, there's four that are willing and able to go. It's a start, I suppose.'

'It's the whole point, isn't it, Dora,' said Mary. 'They can't do without us. They say we shouldn't have the vote because we're too silly to understand big questions, because we can't be soldiers, and suchlike nonsense. But really the truth is they're afraid. Afraid what it would mean for them if we got treated equally with them. We might not do their bidding quite so readily.'

Dora nodded. 'Think of them coming in and finding there's not a meal on the table.'

'The washing not done.'

'The baby crying.'

The girls clutched each other, laughing.

'Stop, you've given me a stitch,' said Mary after a moment, wiping tears of laughter from her eyes with a hanky. 'I can just see my uncle's face if he knew … you know, he thinks that women have smaller brains than men. An' the worst of it is – me aunt agrees with him!' She rolled her eyes.

'Aye – I've heard a lot of them say the same,' Dora said. 'But your mam doesn't think that, does she?'

'No,' said Mary. 'I really wish she could vote. She deserves it. If things were different, I'm sure she'd join the branch. I wish – oh, I wish I could go to London, fight for her. Next time maybe.'

'I know, I feel the same,' said Dora. Her mam should have the right to vote too. She had more up top and was more capable than most men Dora knew.

If only she could carry forward the fight for her – all the way to Parliament. If she were older now … Dora sighed, clenching her hands tightly. She wanted to do more than just attend meetings and hand out leaflets. Deeds, not words, that was their motto after all.

'If it were just me, I'd not care,' she heard Mary say suddenly. 'I'd go to prison willingly. But I don't want to make things harder for Mam and my sisters.'

The girls were silent, each lost in her own thoughts. A harsh sound broke into their' reverie.

'There's the buzzer,' sighed Mary. 'Time to get back.'

Chapter Eighteen

The living room of the Keys' home on Regent Place was packed. Mrs Key was pacing up and down, hands clasped behind her back. Dora wished she'd sit down or at least stand still. The house shook suddenly as a train rumbled past. The women jumped, and someone gave a nervous laugh. Dora rubbed her foot, which had gone to sleep. How long had they been sitting there? How long before they got any news? She stood up, stamping her foot to wake it up, and hobbled over to the window. She pressed her face to the pane. It was night, and the gaslights cast eerie shadows on to the street below. She looked back into the room. Mam and Mrs Pinnance were talking to each other in low voices. Strange how they all felt the need to speak in whispers. Another woman, Mrs Hall, who lived near the Thewlises on the Leeds road, was pretending to drink her tea. Dora's cup was untouched on the table next to her.

Downstairs the bell jangled sharply and every face turned towards the door. Dora clenched her hands into fists. News from London. It had to be. Nice Mr Key got up heavily and Dora heard the stairs creak as he walked slowly downstairs. Mr Key was blind and how he found his way around was a miracle to Dora. But he did. He had even toured Europe playing the organ. A staunch socialist too; she had seen him speaking from a wagon in town on Sundays. Who was it at the door then? Dora couldn't wait to find out. She pulled up the window and leaned out, shivering as a blast of icy air whistled past her into the room.

'Shut that window, lass,' someone in the room objected, but Dora took no notice. She craned her head out as far as she could and looked down. She could see Mr Key standing in the street below.

'Telegram,' she heard a boy say.

'Telegram,' she called back jubilantly into the room. She shut the window and returned to her seat. But how hard it was to sit calmly and patiently. How long it seemed before she heard Mr Key's step on the stair again. The door opened. Mr Key entered the room and silently held out the telegram to his wife. How steady Mrs Key's hands were, thought Dora. Hers would be shaking with the weight of such important news. There was a moment's complete silence as Mrs Key scanned the telegram. Dora did not take her eyes from her face. What did the telegram say? Why does she not tell us? she thought impatiently.

'A wire from the front,' Mrs Key said calmly at last. No one moved, it was as if even the room was holding its breath, Dora thought.

A smile broke on Mrs Key's face. 'There have been arrests,' she said. 'We have done well.'

Who? Who? thought Dora. Tell us who! 'Miss Beever and Mrs Sykes are amongst those arrested. Miss Christabel Pankhurst –'

A great cheer rose up drowning the rest of Mrs Key's words. Women punched the air, embraced each other. Dora felt herself half smothered in a big hug. Two of their own had been arrested for the cause. Mam's eyes looked very bright, Dora thought, and she was blinking them very fast as if there were tears in them. She almost felt like crying herself.

Bit by bit news filtered through. Two of the leaders including their own Mary Gawthorpe had also been arrested. Bail had been arranged for the arrested suffragettes by Mr Frederick Pethick-Lawrence, the barrister husband of Emmeline Pethick-Lawrence, the WSPU's Treasurer.

In the morning the suffragettes would return to the magistrate's court to be sentenced, Mrs Key told them. As more news came in the women sobered up a bit. The police had been heavy-handed, some said. Mounted police had even tried to ride down the women as they marched on Parliament. Women had had their hands torn roughly from the railings. They'd find out more in the morning. The papers were bound to be full of it, thought Dora, as she lay in bed, vainly trying to sleep later that night. The rest they'd learn from Ellen Beever and Annie Sykes when they returned. When might that be? A week – or more? They wouldn't be imprisoned for longer, would they? It was their first time.

'They were brave, weren't they?' she heard Evie say quietly.

Dora nodded, forgetting that in the dark Evie couldn't see her face. By this time tomorrow, she thought, Annie Sykes and Ellen Beever would have been bundled off in a police van to Holloway gaol along with all the other prisoners. They'd be offered the chance to pay a fine but Dora felt certain they'd not take it. Few suffragette prisoners did. The more that were locked up, the better the publicity for the cause.

'How could they do it? – willingly to go to prison.' Dora could hear the shudder in her sister's voice.

She pillowed her head on her arms. She felt as if she could almost hear the rattle of the prison van – the Black Maria – as it took the women to Holloway gaol. 'Rise up women, rise up,' she whispered to herself. 'And the cause goes marching on. Glory, glory, hallelujah.'

Because it would – whatever happened this time. But then to hear the heavy gates slam shut behind you. It'd take a deal of courage to go willingly into that place. Dora had seen a picture of Holloway gaol. It looked more like a medieval fortress than a prison, to her mind. Turrets and all. Aye it'd take courage. But they had it – plenty of it. She rolled over on to her side and stared into the dark. How'd she ever be able to sleep?

Anyone who didn't know that Huddersfield women – their own Huddersfield women – had gone to London to fight for the cause would know soon enough. It would come as a shock to some! Dora smiled to herself and shut her eyes. They'd lit a match to a flame this night all right – those valiant Huddersfield women.

By morning the news was all over town. Dora rifled though the pile of papers on the table. Mam must have bought a copy of every paper she could lay her hands on. Pictures of bedraggled women manhandled by big burly policemen stared up at her from the front pages. It had been a wet afternoon in London.

'You've seen the news then,' her father said coming into the kitchen. He put down the hod of coal and began to shovel it vigorously on to the fire. He sounded angry. 'Women ridden down by mounted police. Torn away from railings.' He shook his head disgustedly.

'Aye, but 56 women arrested. 56!' boomed a jubilant voice.

Dora turned her head to see her mother on the stairs, Arthur over her shoulder. 'The most ever taken. And most of them ordinary working people too.'

'That will make the government sit up and take notice, won't it, Mam?' said Dora eagerly.

Her mother set Arthur down. 'Aye, it will. It will help spread the message. The government will have to stop pretending it's just a few posh women wanting their rights. The cause will soon be won. Mark my words.' She looked round at her family, as if daring any of them to disagree. But who could? thought Dora. Her heart felt full – too full to speak. Mam was right. That would show them. Women would not be silenced.

Chapter Nineteen

'Off home now, girls?' asked Dora as she and Mary caught up with Flo and Evie in the yard.

'Yes, like you should be too,' said Flo. 'What's that you're holding?' she said suspiciously as Dora whipped her hand behind her back.

'Oh that!' Dora opened her fist, and looked down at the piece of chalk lying on her palm as if she was surprised to see it there. 'Looks like a piece of chalk to me.'

'Now, listen, Dora,' said Flo, firmly.

'Say what you've got to say,' Dora said. 'I'm listening.'

But Flo saw an obstinate look spread over her sister's face. She sighed. She felt sure that Dora would take precious little heed of anything she had to say. 'You be careful now,' she said. 'You know what people have been saying since the raid on Parliament.'

'Yes, I do,' said Dora. 'The WSPU have opened up a lot of new branches on the back of it. All over the country women are responding to the call!'

'You know very well what I mean. Plenty of folk aren't happy about it – that raid – and are making their feelings known,' Flo said sternly.

She sounded like her grandmother, Dora thought. 'What have they to do with me?' she said. 'We need to stand together. Now. Shoulder to shoulder.'

'I don't want to hear you've been put in prison for chalking slogans on the pavement. You got to be careful. Why – even the neighbours are asking questions. Mrs Brown –'

'Oh her. You don't want to listen to her,' interrupted Dora. 'The old busybody.'

She hated it when Flo came over all big-sisterly. Why must she talk to her as if she was a child?

'I'll see you later,' she said. 'I won't get put in prison, so don't fret. Don't eat all the tea. Nighty night, Mary!'

She skipped away from them. Honestly, the fuss they made. She was only going to write a notice or two down about the next meeting. Who'd care? All right, they had been advised not to chalk pavements on their own, but she could look after herself.

She could hear steps. Light steps, running steps, mirroring her own. It sounded as if … as if someone was following her. But what did it matter? She hadn't done anything – yet. Probably just one of those blooming sisters of hers. Dora tossed her head. She wasn't going to let anyone stop her from doing what she had to do.

93

The steps were getting closer.

'Dora, stop! It's only me, Mary!' a voice said breathlessly.

Dora whirled round.

'Mary! What are you doing here?' Her eyes narrowed suspiciously. 'Did those sisters of mine put you up to minding me?'

'No, but I'm coming with you,' Mary puffed as she caught up with Dora. 'You shouldn't chalk pavements on your own. It isn't safe.'

Dora shook her head. 'No, Mary. I can't let you. What if we get caught? If we get put away your uncle will tell the police to throw away the key!'

'We won't get caught,' said Mary. 'Because I'm going to watch out for you while you write the words.'

Dora laughed and slipped her arm through Mary's. She was a true friend.

'Evie and Flo are right, you know,' said Mary.

'I know,' said Dora soberly. She'd only said what she had to annoy her sisters. Their fussing got on her nerves. She could take care of herself. But she knew as well as them that not everyone in the town had been pleased to discover that Huddersfield women had taken part in the suffragette raid on Parliament. From the way some of them talked, you'd think they were a coven of witches. If anything it had made Dora more determined. But if she was to be arrested, she'd make sure it was outside Parliament, not chalking a few words on a pavement.

'Where are we going to do it?' said Mary. 'Here will do,' said Dora, stopping short. They were near the top of Northumberland Street. The meeting was to take place in the Friendly and Trades Club, further down the street. Yes, Dora thought, satisfied. This was a good place to do it. The post office was a few steps away. They weren't far from the market here either. Lots of people would see what she'd written. Indeed, there were plenty of people out on the street now.

She grinned at her friend. 'Ready, Mary?'

Mary looked doubtful. 'There's an awful lot of people around,' she said, nodding at the men and women strolling down the street. A tram full of shoppers turned into the road.

'Good,' said Dora firmly. 'Then they'll see what I've written. Get them along to a meeting. That's what I'm here for.'

'But –' began Mary.

'I'm not doing it in a back street where no one will see it!' Dora exclaimed.

She crouched down, and began to write rapidly, in big letters.

Mary stood close to Dora and looked around warily. A few people had already stopped to see what Dora was doing – lads and men mostly, as usual. One of the men came up close and bent down. After all, a girl on her knees chalking the pavement was not a sight you saw every day in Huddersfield! He shook his head disapprovingly, and ambled off, muttering.

Men, thought Mary. They had been pleased enough to see the suffragettes when they wanted to get the Liberal out, but it was another matter when women asked for the right to vote…

'Eh you!' a voice hollered. 'What do you think you're doing?'

Mary jerked her head round. A man was staring at them, on the other side of the street. A big burly man dressed in … Mary swallowed. He was in uniform and had a helmet on his head.

'Stop that!' the policeman shouted, breaking into a run.

'Dora, stop. Police!' she hissed, bending down close to her friend. 'Rub it out.'

'Not on your life!' said Dora, getting quickly to her feet. 'Where is he?' she asked. 'Is he far away?'

'Not very…'

'Then let's be going…'

'Run?'

'Yes!'

The girls fell back against the wall laughing. 'Oh, I didn't know I could run as fast as that,' Dora gasped, clutching her side.

Mary tiptoed to the corner of the street and looked round carefully. There was no sign of their pursuer.

'He's gone,' she said. 'Do you think he saw our faces?'

Dora shook her head. 'Only the backs of our heads.' She straightened up.

'Let's get home,' she said. 'Come back and have a cuppa.'

'No, I'd best get on home.' Mary hesitated. She seemed to be spending more and more time at the Thewlises and she felt bad that she couldn't return their hospitality. 'I wish I could ask you round,' she said, 'but…'

'Your uncle wouldn't like it. I know,' said Dora.

They walked slowly down the road. 'Let's go by the canal,' said Dora. 'Just in case…'

'Just in case…'

Chapter Twenty

'What now?' said Mary. She'd popped by for tea and found the family poring over the papers.

Dora pulled her friend aside. 'There's a rumour that they will call on us mill girls next time there's a raid on Parliament,' she hissed. 'That's the message we've had back from the leaders. We'll give the police a taste of their medicine. Soon sort 'em, send 'em running.' Her black eyes looked very bright.

Mary stared at her friend. '*Us* mill girls,' Dora had said. 'You're not thinking of going?' she said, startled.

'We'll see what we'll see,' said Dora. 'We'll find out more at the meeting.'

Mary looked over at Dora's parents. Would they allow their daughter to take part in another London crusade, should there be one, which Dora seemed very certain there would be? Her mother now. Mary glanced at Eliza Thewlis's strong face. She knew what power Dora's mam had to persuade, sway people to her will. Dora too had a will of her own. But she was still so young. Mary felt afraid for her friend suddenly. Dora is a sensible girl, she told herself. But she couldn't help worrying. All the excitement had turned Dora's head.

She looked up at Dora to find her eyes on her.

'I know what you're thinking,' said Dora. 'My parents would be right behind me, never fear.' She spoke confidently.

'But aren't you forgetting something,' said Mary. 'The branch would never accept you –'

'It's early days,' said Dora, snapping her fingers. 'I'm not saying anything now and mind you don't either.'

She wandered off to the table. Mary watched as she said something to her mother. Eliza laughed and put an arm around her daughter's shoulders.

Mary shrugged. There was after all nothing more she could say. Events had caught them all up in some wild dizzying whirl and who knew where and how any of them would get put down.

Chapter Twenty-one

'It is time to rise and assail our opponents' position,' boomed Eliza Thewlis from the platform. 'Prisoners have been taken from Huddersfield and there are others ready to go and suffer if another batch is needed.'

Sitting a few rows back in the hall, Dora felt very proud. Her mam – chairing a meeting of hundreds! Next to her mother sat Mrs Key, the branch secretary, and several other women including Annie Kenney. There too was their own Ellen Beever who had recently been released from prison. Dora was agog to hear what she would have to say. Mrs Key was speaking now. After protesting about the police's brutal treatment of the suffragettes she called on the government to adopt Mr Dickenson's private member's bill. The bill wouldn't give all women the vote, but it was a start. Next Ellen Beever rose to her feet.

'I was asked how I liked prison,' she said. 'I told them I didn't go to like but to look and condemn because it was wrong. Aye it was wrong,' she said firmly, in answer to some 'go along with yous' from hecklers who had slipped in somewhere near the back of the hall. 'I was charged with obstructing the pathway,' she went on. 'But it was a false charge. I could 'ave walked right into the House of Commons and taken my message to the government there and then, but there were a few people obstructing me from doing so – a lot of officers and the mob, and some mounted police and then we were run away with and had a ride in a Black Maria…'

Her words were interrupted by a burst of laughter. When it had died down, Ellen Beever went on, 'I tell you, women could not do better than force their way into Parliament and have a proper spring cleaning … of their injustices.' A roar of delighted laughter and applause broke out, and, bowing slightly, Ellen Beever sat down. She was a born speaker, Dora thought, wiping tears of laughter from her cheeks. She turned to Mary, who was sitting by her side. A wide grin split Mary's face.

'She's a tonic, that Ellen Beever,' she said.

Annie Kenney stood up. All faces were upturned to the slight figure with the large eyes that seemed to speak as passionately as her words. The hurt she felt at injustice and wrong showed in her face, Dora thought, gazing at her wide-eyed.

'Well, I'm glad to find that a *man* has had the courage of his convictions and brought forth a bill for the women's vote. I ask the government to adopt it. We're often blamed', she said seriously, 'for our methods but our mothers and grandmothers fought for nearly 50 years – *50 years…*' She paused – you could have heard a pin drop in that hall, Dora thought – 'And so we, their grandchildren, must adopt different methods. I've been told – we've all been told this I'm sure – that there are more important things for Parliament to spend its time on, like children having enough to eat, the plight of the unemployed, but we want the vote to help these good causes along, and a bit faster too than has been the case up till now.'

Her eyes strayed over the hundreds of faces turned up to her. 'There's a woman in this room,' she said, 'whose sister works for 58 hours a week for three shillings and sixpence. I tell you, if women had the vote they'd use it better than the men, aye and make sure that women no longer have to work for sweatshop wages like that.'

She stopped and her gaze travelled slowly over her audience again. 'I will never be satisfied,' she said, 'until I see one thousand Lancashire and Yorkshire women clattering in their clogs on the floor of the House of Commons.' Mary smiled and glanced at Dora. But Dora didn't smile back. She was leaning forward, head on hand, listening intently. She looked, Mary thought, as if a spell had been cast on her. Mary felt a sudden chill. She wished that Annie hadn't said those words. Dora didn't need any encouraging.

One thousand Lancashire and Yorkshire women clattering

in their clogs on the floor of the House of Commons, Dora thought. Her eyes shone. One thousand Lancashire and Yorkshire women in Parliament! What a picture that conjured up!

'Wasn't it marvellous what Mrs Mitchell said,' said Mary after the next speaker had sat down. 'Turning round what men say. That their brains are heavier than ours, which makes them slower thinkers.'

Dora was still thinking about Annie's speech. 'Aye, but did you hear what Annie said,' she said excitedly. '"We will fight until the victory has been won."' And we mill workers will make sure of that, she thought determinedly to herself.

She turned back to the platform. Speeches over, Eliza was inviting questions from the audience. Dora heard a man say loudly, 'And you bunch of rampaging women – I read what you did outside the Parliament, you're a disgrace, you are – shaming all decent, law-abiding women – and you, you really think you'd make a better job of running things than what we 'ave, do yer?'

'Aye we do,' said Eliza, smiling. 'Next.'

'I've not done. I've a lot more to say.'

'You've made your point. And made it very clearly. I'm sure we've all taken it to heart,' said Eliza. A titter ran through the audience. 'But,' she went on, calmly but firmly, 'there are others here who would like to put a question too.'

'Who'll do the cooking and cleaning if you lot get the vote? I can just see it now. You women – you were born to be men's helpmates, not run the country – an' if your rampaging about is a taste of what we can expect –' The man's voice rose angrily.

A chorus of hissing and boos broke out.

'Would the gentleman kindly sit down,' said Eliza.

'Aye, sit down,' several voices cried, male voices amongst them. Dora swivelled round to see the man pulled down by those on either side of him. He folded his arms and smirked. A man sitting in the row behind clapped him on the back.

'Some men,' muttered Dora. 'Still, what do we care what an idiot like that thinks.' She turned to Mary, expecting her to agree. But Mary's face was white, and she seemed to be trying to make herself disappear.

'Whatever's the matter?' Dora whispered, startled.

'It's 'im – me uncle,' Mary whispered back.

'What! Whoever let him in?'

'Whoever let everyone else in, I suppose,' said Mary wearily. 'Oh, I knew I shouldn't have come. I shouldn't have come.' She sank further down in her seat and put her head in her hands. 'Pray that he doesn't see us.'

'Are you sure it's him? Why would he come here – to a suffragette meeting?'

'To make his views known. You heard him. He hates us and all we stand for.'

There were a fair number of men in the audience – Dora's father amongst them – but not all of them were sympathetic to the cause, that was already clear.

'What if he sees me?' said Mary desperately. 'What if he has seen me already?'

'Mary, I'm sure he hasn't,' said Dora. 'Anyway,' she shrugged. 'If he has, you can pretend you're here to protest too. There are bound to be some protesters amongst the women here. Not all of them support the cause – as we both know.'

Her words didn't comfort Mary. 'He'll never believe that.'

Dora laid a hand on Mary's arm. It felt tight and tense. 'Don't worry,' she said comfortingly. She glanced round. She couldn't see the man. Had he left?

'I shouldna have come,' muttered Mary again.

Dora put up a hand. 'Ssh. Listen.' On the platform the leaders were asking for volunteers – delegates willing to come forward to take part in the next crusade to the House of Commons, in two weeks' time, if MPs tried to stop the progress of the Dickenson bill through Parliament.

She looked round at the women sitting near her. Some of them were conferring, others looked away or down at their feet. Who would answer the call? Who could resist such a plea? And she herself … She looked up at the platform and straight into her mother's eyes. 'Will you go, Dora? Will you go for me, for the cause?' her mother's eyes seemed to be asking her. Or was she imagining it?

There was a large burst of applause. The meeting was over. The speakers began to descend from the platform.

'What am I to do? He'll kill me, or throw me out, mebbe even throw us all out, if he finds me here.' Mary's desperate whisper reminded Dora of her friend's plight.

'Just wait. I'll think of something,' she said. Was the man still in the hall? she wondered. Could they make a dash for it? She'd liked to have turned round to see, but the hall was fast emptying and she didn't want to draw attention to them. Mary was sitting next to her, rigid as a stone. What should they do? They couldn't sit there for ever.

'My hat and coat!' Dora said, suddenly. 'Here. Put them on. I'll take your shawl, then we'll go up to Mam at the front. He won't dare go near the speakers. Mam would give him a piece of her mind if he did.' Hastily she began to unpin her hat. She shoved it into Mary's lap and shrugged off her coat. Then she stood up. 'Give it a minute. Then follow me up to the platform.'

There was still a gaggle of people talking near the platform. As Dora made her way up to them, she wondered how many had handed in their names for the next London crusade.

Her mother was talking rapidly to Mrs Key, who seemed a trifle distracted, Dora thought. Annie Kenney stood nearby. She smiled when she saw Dora. 'Why, it's Miss Thewlis, isn't it?' she said.

'That was a grand speech you made, Miss Kenney,' Dora said shyly. 'Have there been many names handed in yet?'

'Four so far.'

Only four – after that speech. Dora was dumbfounded. '*Four* – out of so many?'

Annie laughed. 'We've time yet to coax the others. And several have said to me – quietly, mind – that they might come forward. I think – well – some of them are not sure what their families might think. Or how they'd manage without them.' She gave a wry smile.

I've no husband to demand his tea, or children to take care of, Dora's thoughts tumbled incoherently through her mind. She looked straight into Annie Kenney's eyes. 'I could go,' she said clearly, 'if more are needed. I'd like to – I'm a mill worker.' She blushed, stumbling over her words in her eagerness. 'You said you wanted mill workers to join the crusade, didn't you?'

'We'll send big strong mill girls from up north, next time,' Annie had said. She, Dora, wasn't that big, but she would fight, if called upon to. She'd not give up.

Out of the corner of her eye she saw Mrs Key's eyebrows go up. Had she heard her? Annie looked seriously at her. Please don't say I'm too young, thought Dora.

'You've thought about this, then?' Annie said quietly. 'It means arrest… prison…'

'Aye, a lot. Aye, I've thought about it a lot. It's no last-minute decision,' declared Dora.

She glanced round to see that Mary had squeezed herself into a group near them. That was something. There were few people left in the hall now, but there were some men still talking near the door. Their backs were turned to them, but what if Mary's uncle was amongst them? What if he turned round and saw Mary?

'Miss Kenney, would you mind if we talked outside? My friend –' she nodded at Mary – 'has a relative here who is none too friendly to the cause. It would be better if he didn't see her here.'

Annie looked sympathetically at Mary. 'Of course. Come along then.' She put out an arm and shepherded the two girls to the door. As she moved off, so did the others.

'He'll not see you now,' Dora whispered to Mary. 'There's safety in crowds.'

'There's many who don't understand what we're trying to do,' she heard Annie say to Mary when they were outside. 'Or how important it is for us all.'

Dora looked over to where her mother and father stood. Her mother was talking to Mrs Mitchell. Dad was listening. Most of the others had drifted away. Dad was the only man she could still see. It was not a night for lingering. A brisk wind whipped their faces and a few drops of rain spattered down.

'It's a true northern March night,' said Annie, wrapping her shawl more closely around her head.

'Aye, we should be going,' said Dora. 'Mary, I'll walk back part o' the way with you.'

They bade Annie farewell and saw her walk over to Mrs Thewlis and say something. Eliza turned her head and smiled. Mrs Mitchell waved.

'That Mrs Mitchell, did you hear what she said?' said Dora. She laughed. 'Ow men's brains are so heavy that it takes a while to get them moving!'

'An' that we shouldn't have the vote as we can't be soldiers or policemen! Where've I heard that before!' Mary said. She'd perked up a bit, Dora thought, now that they'd put a few yards between them and the hall.

'And how if women had the vote they'd put it to better use than men. Almost anything would be better use,' said Dora.

'Is that so…' a man's voice growled behind them. The two girls started.

'It's 'im,' murmured Mary. 'My uncle.'

'What? How can you be sure?'

'I'm sure of it. Bye, Dora. I'll try and outrun him.'

'Don't look round, run,' whispered Dora. 'You go right, I'll turn left. That'll throw him.'

She clutched Mary's hand briefly then the two ran. Mary soon outstripped Dora. She could run, thought

Dora, as she slipped down a side road. And with an uncle like that, it was just as well.

It was a fair way to Hawthorne Terrace and Dora didn't dare take a direct route home. She dodged up and down alleys and side roads until she could run no more. No one was following her. She leaned back against a wall, breathing heavily. When she had got her breath back she walked slowly along to the main road. If a tram came she'd jump on it, but it would serve her right if it didn't. Poor Mary, Dora thought. If that awful man caught up with her, who knew what trouble she'd be in and it was all her fault. She had encouraged her with all her talk about the cause. She should have left well alone.

Chapter Twenty-two

'I brought your hat and coat,' said Mary. 'Thank you,' Dora murmured, taking them from her. 'And here's your shawl.' They squeezed together through the gate. Dora was desperate to find out what had happened after Mary had run off last night. Mary had said nothing about it – nothing at all. Dora's mind was in turmoil. She'd lain awake for hours at night worrying. Had Mary got home before her uncle, or did he catch up with her? Had he recognised her in the street? And what then? What if he turned them all out of the house? How could she ever forgive herself?

'Uncle did see me,' Mary said suddenly, as they walked across the yard to the weaving shed.

Dora felt a sick feeling grip her stomach. Mary would never have gone to that meeting if she hadn't encouraged her. What kind of trouble had she led her friend into? 'I'm ever so sorry,' said Dora miserably. 'It was my fault…' She couldn't say any more. Her mouth had gone dry.

Mary looked into her friend's distressed face. 'You mustn't blame yourself,' she said, earnestly. 'I wanted to go to the meeting. I truly did. I never thought to see him there.'

'He's not…' Dora licked her dry lips. She couldn't bring herself to say the words. *'He's not turning you out of the house?'*

'It's not as bad as you think. He's forbidden me to 'ave anything to do with the WSPU, but I will one day,' she said defiantly. 'Just as soon as I am able to support myself.'

And when would that be? thought Dora. It wasn't easy for a single woman mill worker to support herself. And when she was married and had a family of her own, what time did she have for herself then?

'He said I was a disgrace, had brought shame on the family,' Mary said suddenly, in a low voice. 'Oh, how I hate him!'

Dora's eyes flashed angrily. She clenched her hands into fists. How dare he say such a thing! 'I hate it,' she burst out suddenly. 'I hate the power men have over our lives. Things will only change for the better when we are treated as men's equals. I've made up my mind,' she said. 'If there is another suffragette crusade, I'll join it. Anyway, I told Annie Kenney I would. You heard what she said last night. She wants one thousand strong Lancashire and Yorkshire mill girls to go to London. We'll soon sort them. We'll get our rights!'

'An',' she went on quickly before Mary could say anything, 'there's nothing you can say, or anyone can say, that will stop me. I'll find a way – somehow. So don't even try!'

Mary smiled at her friend. 'As if anyone could do that!' she said.

Chapter Twenty-three

'How'd you get on, Mam?' asked Dora eagerly.

Her mother unpinned her hat. 'My, but it's a wild day,' she said, tucking up some stray hairs. 'Annie Kenney said she'd seen nowt like it.' She laughed. 'As stormy as the tempers of the husbands whose wives we've coaxed into signing up for the next crusade.' She unbuttoned her coat and sat down wearily. 'We've a way to go still. Annie's got one hundred strong Lancashire lasses ready and willing, but we in Huddersfield lag behind. Shame on us!'

The bill to grant voting rights to a number of women had had its second reading on 8 March but its supporters were no nearer getting it through Parliament. The suffragette march on the House of Commons was to go ahead as planned.

'I'd go, of course, but there's the bairns to mind and the house to run.' Dora handed her mother a cup of tea. She took a sip.

'Daughters should go for their mothers.' She'd heard someone say that, hadn't she? Who else was there to go anyway? Dora thought. Her sisters couldn't or wouldn't.

None of them had signed up for the WSPU. If no one else would then she must. And she had already promised herself and Mary that she would.

'Let me go, Mam,' she said.

The room went very quiet.

Eliza stared at her daughter, as if she couldn't believe what she had just said.

'Dora, lass –' she began.

'I said, let me go, Mam,' interrupted Dora. 'Let me go!' She looked up at her mother. 'I'm quite capable. I understand what I'm fighting for.'

Her mother shook her head. 'There's no call for you to go, child.'

'Child!' burst out Dora. 'Mam, I'm not a child. I'm rising seventeen.'

Eliza regarded her daughter thoughtfully. 'I'll 'ave to talk it over with your father. And the branch will need to give permission too, of course.'

That meant yes! Mam could bend anyone to her will, if she wished it. Dora flung herself at her mother's feet and gripped her knees.

'Careful, you'll spill me tea,' said Eliza. She put her cup down, then leaned forward and took Dora's hands in hers, holding them tightly. 'You know it will mean prison. I'd expect no less of any of mine,' she said seriously.

'Aye, I know,' said Dora stoutly. Others had done it,

so could she. 'It will be an honour to go to prison for the cause. Women ought to have their rights.'

'Gazing into her daughter's determined face Eliza felt very proud. She had brought up her daughter to think for herself and she had no fears that she could not look after herself. And as for her being too young, well, her boy Bill had gone to fight in South Africa when he was scarcely any older than Dora was now. He'd put his life at the service of his country. No one was asking that of Dora. 'But I must speak to your father,' she said again firmly.

Jim folded his arms and regarded his daughter thoughtfully. 'You're too young,' he wanted to say. He glanced at Eliza. She had already told him that Dora had her blessing. How much she had had to do with this decision of Dora's he didn't know. He didn't like to think of his little girl in that dreadful place – Holloway gaol – but who was he to stand in her way? He wasn't surprised either. Dora had been a loyal and devoted member of the new branch. He had no doubt she'd be a credit to the cause. And he knew it was all too true what she'd argued – that she toiled for others' gain and under laws about which she had no say. He couldn't stop her from joining hands with all those other dauntless women fighting for what was only just and right. But she was young, very young.

'There's a lass agreed to go who's not much older than

Dora,' said Eliza as if she'd guessed what was in Jim's mind. 'And she'll be amongst friends. She'll be taken good care of.'

'Mam!' Dora protested. She could take care of herself.

Her father considered. 'I cannot stand against you both,' he said at last, turning to Eliza. 'And I hope it may do some good. But –' as Dora leapt up joyfully and flung her arms around his neck – 'you know that first we will need the agreement of the branch.'

Eliza was looking at the clock. 'If you're sure, Dora, I will tell the committee that you are willing to go to London as a delegate.'

'I am sure,' said Dora solemnly. Her mother put on her coat.

'You're going out now?' said Jim, surprised.

'Well, there's a meeting of the committee tonight. I may as well put it before them now.'

The branch usually gave in to Mam's demands. It was as good as certain that she would go to London. Dora ran up the stairs, two at a time. She couldn't wait to tell her sisters. What a surprise it would be for them!

'You can't be serious,' gasped Flo.

Dora's chin went up.

'Why not? I told Annie Kenney I'd go. *She* didn't try to stop me. Anyway, who else is there to go?' she demanded.

'Mam can't – who'd look after the little 'uns and cook and clean for you all?'

'But why's it got to be you, Dora? You're still only sixteen! Why not one of the other members? And your job, Dora? What about your job?' exclaimed Flo.

'I'll only be gone a week. I'll be back almost before anyone's noticed.' When Annie Kenney had left her job, the overlooker had begged her to return, Dora remembered. And there were plenty of weaving jobs around right now. She'd be all right.

'You're not thinking of –' Flo couldn't get the word out. She looked at Evie for support. Evie shrugged. She knew well enough that once Dora had made up her mind, nothing anyone could say would change it.

'Prison,' put in Dora. She'd say it how it was. No point in pretending she wasn't planning to go to prison like the rest. 'Well what's the point of me going if I just come home again a day later?' she said defiantly. 'We want to get noticed.'

'*You'll* get noticed all right,' said Flo tartly.

'And have you thought what it will be like,' she said. 'Miss Beever told me that she had to make hardened sheets. She only had bread and tea, the bread was hard –'

'And the tea tasted like tin. Aye I know,' said Dora impatiently. 'But she also said she didn't go to prison to like. And anyway, suffragettes are better treated in prison now. We're political prisoners.' She put her hands on her hips and said defiantly, 'I'm going and you can't stop me. Nothing you say will change my mind. I thought you'd understand. We women must stand united.'

'Oh Dora, you're not thinking straight,' Flo groaned, putting her head in her hands.

'I'm doing it for you – for you and Mam. Can't you see that? Dora said passionately. 'Oh, what's the use!'

She turned away from them and sat down on the bed, her back to her sisters. Flo and Evie looked at each other. 'I'm goin' to help with the little 'uns,' Flo said sharply. 'Someone had better. Don't want to leave young Arthur on his own.'

The door slammed. Evie hesitated. Dora still sat there, unmoving. She went up to her and sat down next to her on the bed. Dora shifted away from her. 'Dora,' she said quietly.

'I'm sick of it,' Dora burst out at last.

'Sick of what?' said Evie.

'This!' Dora made a sweep of her arm. 'Ten hours at the loom. Day in, day out, what sort of future is that? But it's not just about me. I want things to be better for all women. For us all. And until we get the vote things won't get better.' She beat the bedclothes with her fists. 'I must do this. Can you not see?'

'I know,' said Evie quietly. Dora laid her head on her

sister's shoulder. Rain was spattering against the window. Outside, the sky was growing dark, but it was still light enough for the sisters to see the tall mill chimneys. 'I do understand,' she said. 'I do. An' you, Dora,' she put an arm round her sister's shoulders and shook them slightly, 'are the one of us to do it. You've got more pluck than the rest of us put together.'

'I am afraid, a bit,' Dora confessed. 'But I couldn't live with myself if I didn't go.'

Nothing daunted her sister, Evie thought. 'You'll make them sit up. I know you will.' She remembered something. 'Has the branch given permission? You'll need that, won't you?'

Dora rubbed her eyes. 'They'll give it all right,' she declared. 'They're a bit short of the thousand Lancashire and Yorkshire women Annie Kenney wants to clatter in their clogs over the floor of the House of Commons.' She smiled ruefully.

'How much short?'

'Eight hundred and ninety-six short,' said Dora. Evie looked at her – and they burst out laughing.

'So you see, what choice have I got!' Dora declared.

Chapter Twenty-four

The little band of women stood on the station platform, smartly dressed in hats and coats. One of them, Ellen Brooke, couldn't keep still. She ran down the platform and peered down the track. A puff of white smoke announced an approaching train. 'It's coming! The train's coming!' she called excitedly.

'Right on time too,' said Mrs Calpin, glancing up at the station clock. 'Must be on our side then.'

The women laughed. With a hiss the big black train came to a chuntering stop. Steam billowed around the women.

Mrs Key looked round at her fellow suffragettes.

'Are you ready, ladies?' Standing a little apart from the others, Dora felt her heart give a big thump. Was she ready? Here it was, the train that was to take her away from home and everything that was familiar to her, on the first stage of their journey south. Her mother and Mrs Key were accompanying them as far as Manchester. There they'd be joined by the mill workers from Lancashire, one hundred strong, Annie Kenney had promised. And then it was on –

to London. And to … Well, whatever else it would be to, it would be an adventure.

Taking a deep breath, Dora picked up her basket and followed the others on to the train. In the basket were packed her clogs and shawl – which she was to wear for the march on Parliament. Though there was only a ten-strong contingent from Huddersfield, Dora knew that this was to be the biggest demonstration the WSPU had ever staged. What would the other passengers think if they knew where they were headed? she thought, grinning to herself suddenly as she made her way into a compartment. They think we're respectable women, like them.

Off on a morning's jaunt to Manchester. 9.33. The train began to draw out of the station. Dora stowed her basket by her feet and settled herself back comfortably in her seat. Mrs Key sat at one end of the compartment. She caught Dora's eye and gave her an encouraging smile. What she really felt about Dora's presence amongst the Huddersfield delegates Dora wasn't sure. When Mam had returned bearing the message that her name had been added to the list of delegates she had been too excited to take in anything more. But she should be grateful, Dora thought. They should all be grateful. In spite of all the persuasion and encouraging words from Annie Kenney and Adela Pankhurst, Huddersfield branch had only managed to get ten together. Ten, out of all those signed up to the branch!

They should be ashamed of themselves, the rest of them!

Dora rubbed the grimy window with her hand and looked out. They had left Huddersfield town behind them now, but she could see tendrils of smoke wind upwards from the mills that dotted the valley. On any other weekday she'd have been at the loom for around three hours by now. It had felt strange to see her father and sisters off to work and be left behind with Mam and the little ones. They had given each other big hugs – all angry words forgotten – and Dora had felt her eyes begin to water. How dear they were to her. How could she bear to leave them? How long would it be before she saw any of them again, she had thought, standing in the doorway staring after them until they were out of sight. Then Mam had called her in and in what seemed no time at all her things were packed and they were on their way to the station.

The train was slowing down. Dora could see big dark imposing buildings ahead – red brick stained with smoke. Manchester, she thought excitedly. She pulled down the window and poked out her head.

'We'll 'ave our breakfast here,' Dora heard her mother say as the train came to a hissing stop. 'Come along, Dora, don't dawdle, we don't want to leave you behind.'

'No indeed,' joked one of the others. 'Our Dora's going to show us how to tackle them policemen.'

'Oh, they'll be bowing down to us, time I've finished

with them,' Dora said airily. The women laughed. Eliza regarded her daughter proudly. Her Dora had more spirit than the rest of them put together, she thought.

Dora had thought she was hungry but when food was put before her she found she could hardly swallow a morsel. Excitement had tied her stomach into knots. And soon they were being whisked off to the station for the noonday train south, but what a difference there was now! If the station had been busy before, now it was heaving. There were women everywhere, most of them gathered on the platform where the London train was to leave from. Lancashire dialects mingled with Yorkshire as women greeted each other. Annie Kenney's one hundred mill workers, Dora thought, seeing a large group of women, shawls over their heads. None of them looked very old, but none was as young as her. So many women gathered together and onlookers staring, cameras flashing, bouquets pressed into the women's hands by eager supporters.

'That's us,' said Eliza, nodding at a group of women standing on the edge of the crowd. Amongst them Dora saw Annie Kenney's slight figure and shining eyes. She was talking animatedly to a man, who was busily jotting her words down in a notebook. A camera flashed. Annie inclined her head and as if she had sensed Dora looking turned and smiled at her.

'You said you'd come – and you have,' she said as Dora

124

and her mother reached her. 'You must be very proud of your daughter,' she said to Eliza.

'Aye I am. Dora knew how hard it would be for me to take part, much though I'd have liked to, and she said at once she'd come. Mind, I'd have expected no less from her.'

'Mam,' Dora murmured, the praise making her cheeks flush with embarrassment.

'You need have no fears about Dora,' said Annie. 'We will take good care of her. Mrs How-Martyn and Mrs Despard will take charge of her in London. Now,' she said, surveying the platform, and gesturing to the women in shawls and clogs. 'What do you think of my army of women?'

'It's grand, Miss Kenney,' breathed Dora. She'd not been sure what to expect, but it wasn't this. There was hardly room to move on the platform now – and to think of it. They were all suffragettes like her, all about to fight like her for women's right to vote.

All too soon it was time to go. The women bade farewell to each other. Kisses and hugs and whispered words of encouragement. Eliza pulled Dora close and said to her, 'Remember why you are going and what for. Do your duty by the WSPU. I'm proud of you, dear child. Very proud,' she muttered quickly, before turning away hastily. Dora watched wistfully as her mother's back disappeared into the crowds of spectators. She felt a lump rise in her throat.

She was on her own now. Home seemed very far away. She turned back to the train.

'Hurry up, Dora, or we'll go without you,' young Ellen Brooke shouted, leaning out of the window and beckoning to her. Hastily Dora mounted the steps to the train, last of the Huddersfield women to board.

Just before the door slammed behind her, a woman standing on the platform called up to her, 'Lass, here lass, take these and bring down a policeman for me!' She pushed a bunch of flowers into Dora's hands.

Dora laughed her thanks and waved it over her head. 'Aye I will. A dozen if I can.'

A few people laughed and clapped. Clutching her posy, Dora made her way into the compartment where her friends sat. A woman shifted up for her. Outside the guard blew his whistle and waved the spectators back. As the train pulled slowly out of the station Dora could see the supporters and friends who had come to see them off, running alongside the packed carriages, waving and cheering. The train was gathering speed. The spectators stopped running, but she could still see their hankies waving. Now the train had left them far behind, small figures walking away down the platform to the station exit. The women leant back in their seats and smiled at each other. They were off – to do and dare for the vote. And what a grand send-off it had been!

Chapter Twenty-five

Inside Caxton Hall Dora heard the sonorous chimes of Big Ben strike the hour. One. Two. Three. Four. As if it was a signal, the doors of the hall were flung open and out tore the first battalion of suffragettes into the bright sunshine. Dora could hardly keep her seat. How far would they get? she wondered, craning her head round. The whole area around the hall was bristling with police. The women had even heard rumours that they'd turn hosepipes on to them to try and scatter them. The first raid was being led by indomitable Miss Milne, who had already been to prison for the cause.

Before the meeting had begun Dora had walked down Caxton Street to the Palace of Westminster to see the route they would march down later. Along with others she had stood and looked at the great buildings. Some of the women paraded up and down in front of the House of Commons, exciting much comment among spectators and tourists strolling around the square. But Dora had stood and stared up at the great building where the mother of all parliaments was housed. Here it was – the British parliament, the cradle of democracy. But how could it be called that when half the population had no right to vote? And how big and grand and aloof it seemed. How far and remote from the world of the mills and moors she came from. Suddenly Dora felt very small and insignificant. How would they, how *could* they, make the men who sat inside those buildings listen to them? 'We will, we must,' she whispered desperately to herself, feeling her courage begin to seep away.

She must stand firm – shoulder to shoulder with her comrades, for the sake of women everywhere. She must not fail them. 'Give me a spark of nature's fire...' she muttered to herself. 'They will listen. We will make them!' She thought of all that the suffragettes had achieved. Deeds, not words. Aye, deeds, not words. She stared up at the Houses of Parliament defiantly. What was it, after all, just a pile of bricks? No, it was more – a symbol of their oppression that they were chipping away at. She and the other women – aye, they would break down the barrier that separated them from the lawmakers – and force them to bend to their will.

And now, here she was, sitting in the hall surrounded by hundreds of women, all fearless and all as ready as her to face imprisonment, if called on to do so, if it would take them one step nearer getting women the vote. She craned her head round to look up at the gallery. Men

were allowed to sit there if they paid for the privilege –
but they weren't allowed in the body of the hall. Some of
them were on their feet, she saw, scribbling down what the
speakers were saying. She'd read all about it in the papers
in the morning. Or would she? She might be on her way
to prison then. Well, let all the people read what they were
saying and doing here, tomorrow. Let them be as fired up
by their leaders' words as she was – and every other woman
present. In front of them on the platform sat the leaders
of the movement, the banners of the WSPU erect behind
them. Mrs Pankhurst was up there of course, and her fiery
daughter Christabel. How passionionately Christabel had
spoken! And there too was Mrs Pethick-Lawrence, Mrs
Martel and Mrs Despard, who – elderly though she was
– had been imprisoned for her part in the last raid. And
there too was Annie Kenney, wearing a shawl and clogs,
like her and many others in the hall.

A clamour of noisy shouts interrupted the
speech-making. Bruised and battered, suffragettes were
limping back into the hall. Heads turned round. News?
What news? Urgent whispers ran up and down the rows of
women swiftly followed by an outbreak of cheering.

'Miss Milne has been arrested,' someone said to Dora's
group. 'Police advanced from all quarters, but the women
were too much for them.' She laughed delightedly. 'They've
had to call for reinforcements. Twenty arrests already!'

How could anyone sit quietly after that! Dora felt the excitement rise all around her. If you put a match to it, she thought, what a conflagration there would be! That very afternoon they were going to make their claims known to Parliament.

'We must go now,' said Annie Kenney, her voice ringing through the packed hall, 'And show the government what we really feel – that they are hypocrites and cowards to deny us the vote!'

The women cheered. They were to be sent out like soldiers into the field of battle.

Mrs Pankhurst stood up. She had a piece of paper in her gloved hand. Dora held her breath. 'I put the resolution to you,' said Mrs Pankhurst in her beautiful voice.

The meeting, she said, was indignant at the Prime Minister's refusal to grant time to discuss Mr Dickenson's bill which would give women the right to vote. Yet he had declared his conviction that it was right they should have it, so – let him introduce a measure to that effect.

Her eyes rested on the women sitting in front of her. 'I propose', she continued, 'that the resolution be taken at once to Parliament.'

Dora thought the cheers that greeted this proposal would lift off the roof.

'Rise up, rise up women,' came the cry from the platform.

'We will – now,' shouted back Dora and a thousand other voices.

'And who, out of this meeting, will undertake the duty of carrying this resolution to the Prime Minister, if the meeting so desires?'

'I will,' came a resolute voice from the centre of the hall. The cheers that rose at those simple words! A woman stood up.

'Who is she?' Dora bawled in the ear of one of her companions.

'Why – that's Viscountess Harberton,' the woman shouted back over the din. A viscountess, in their midst. Dora's eyes grew wide.

'I will take it to the Prime Minister if the meeting wishes me to,' she heard Lady Harberton say. 'It will be an honour.'

'Lady Harberton will lead the way,' called Mrs Pankhurst from the platform. 'To Westminster, women! To the street, and form yourselves into line behind Lady Harberton.'

Dora leapt to her feet. She could sit still no longer. She must be part of that great procession – and fight her way into the Lobby of the House of Commons itself, as Christabel had demanded of them.

She pushed eagerly through the mass of women, all of whom had the same thought in mind. One of the younger Lancashire mill hands seized her arm. 'Join us!' she said. 'You're one of us, aren't you?'

'Aye, I'm a mill worker too, but I'm from Yorkshire,' Dora said.

'We'll forget that for now,' her companion said, laughing. Behind them women were grabbing each other's arms, all as determined as Dora to be a part of the procession. Those who didn't take part now would follow on later, replacing those who were arrested or who returned to the hall to rest and lick their wounds.

The door was flung open. There was not a cloud to be seen in the sky. A glorious day for a glorious cause, thought Dora, as she stepped into line halfway back in the procession.

But why weren't they moving forward? What was holding them up? 'No one can move for the police. There's a wall of them ahead,' said one of the women next to Dora, who had nipped out of line to have a look. 'Reinforcements,' muttered another. 'Aye, found the last lot too much for them. An' we'll show them too,' said Dora stoutly. 'We'll find a way through.'

'You must stop where you are. You cannot march in procession. You must walk singly and quietly.' The police inspector's words carried back to Dora and her companions.

'I didn't hear that,' said Dora.

'Nor did her ladyship,' said her companion. 'Look!' She pointed. Dora stared round the sea of heads ahead of her. Ignoring the inspector's command, Lady Harberton was striding onwards, skirts flapping round her ankles. She waved the resolution in her hand so that it could be seen clearly. 'Rise up, women. Follow me – onwards – to Westminster.' The line of suffragettes began to shuffle forwards.

'Madam! You can go no further,' the inspector said loudly.

'Oh yes, but we will,' answered Lady Harberton in a ringing voice. 'We are going to the House of Commons. We must. And we will.'

She turned and shouted to the women behind her, 'Rise up. Rise up, women.' It sounded like a battle cry. A call to arms!

The women immediately behind Lady Harberton pushed forward again.

'Votes for women!' Dora heard all around her mingled with shouted orders from the police. 'Votes for women!'

Still a long way back from the leaders, Dora saw the women far ahead of her scatter. Some seemed to have escaped the police and were running down the street.

'Bit of a scrap,' commented one of Dora's companions.

'Hold fast, women!' She couldn't see Lady Harberton now, but at least they were moving forwards, their clogs rattling on the hard London pavements. Dora blinked as they came out into the sunlight. Police seemed to be everywhere, arms waving, shouting orders, blowing whistles.

'Break them up, lads! Break them up!' bawled the inspector.

A line of around fifteen or more constables was chasing a group of suffragettes down an alley. Another line of policemen marched up in their place.

'Grasp arms,' a woman's voice called loudly above the melee. 'Form into groups. Five or six abreast.' Dora felt a hand grasp her arm.

'Link arms,' put in another Lancashire voice breathlessly, taking Dora's other arm. 'They'll find it harder to separate us. Ready, women! March!'

Arms firmly linked, they were moving forwards. They were very close to the police now. Dora saw them advance, a line of black uniforms and helmets.

'Rise up! Votes for women,' shouted Dora. 'Come on,' she bawled at her companions, plunging forwards into the fray. The police were all around them now. Big burly men, twice her size, uniforms buttoned up to their chins, helmets pressed down close on their heads. Spectators cheered the women on. Some even leapt into the scrimmage alongside them. The women surged across the road to the other side. Then it was back again. Dora felt her shawl slip down around her shoulders. Her arms felt as if they were being tugged out of their sockets. If only she could let go, but to let go was to give up.

They were making progress. But it was too slow.

'When we see Westminster Abbey, we're nearly there,' someone nearby puffed.

'Know London well, do you?' gasped Dora. Ahead she could see some of the suffragettes being marched off the field of battle. A large number of their comrades followed them, like a guard of honour. That was it. That was what she should do. Follow the arrested women, pretend to march quietly until the prisoners were hustled into vans. Then make a run for it. She pulled away from the others and slipped into the ranks of women.

Earlier that afternoon, she recalled, the first party of women had sallied out to be repulsed by the police. That, thought Dora, had been the skirmish before the main battle. Battle had been joined now – with a vengeance. Whistles blew near her. The police were on to them. Breaking away the women began to run, swerving past the pursuing police. Dimly, Dora caught sight of a wagonette pulling up nearby and saw several Lancashire mill girls jump nimbly down. They ran headfirst into the crowd of women struggling to reach the House of Commons.

'Rise up. Votes for women!' one of them shouted as she ducked round a policeman. Dora laughed. One hundred strong and burly mill girls, Annie had demanded. She'd got that – and more. Must have played a trick on the wagon driver to get him to take them right up to the head of the procession like that! Just look at his face – eyes popping nearly out of his head. And there were plenty more spectators watching the women struggle to make their way to Parliament. Men and boys in caps, the sort who came to gawp at the suffragettes at those meetings back in Huddersfield. A lot of them were leaping into the crowd. Just an entertainment for most of them. A bit of fun. But for the women, it was a deadly struggle. A life and death struggle. No longer would women let themselves be treated as mere chattels or childbearers. They would have their rights!

Dora saw a woman cling to a railing. A policeman bent over her, trying to dislodge her fingers. And he was twice as big and broad as she was, Dora thought delightedly. They would make the papers, all right. A horde of spectators had gathered nearby to watch the struggle. The traffic in the square had come to a standstill. Men hooted their motor horns, people were clambering out of their cars and carriages to watch the battle. Dora laughed quietly to herself to see how many constables there were attempting to control the women. All those constables – and big strapping men they were too – needed to control a bevy of women half their size.

Old Palace Yard. She was nearly there. In front of her now was the House of Commons itself. Could she force her way in, enter the Lobby? Wouldn't that be something. In the February raid fifteen women had done just that. Dora could see the headlines. 'Sixteen-year-old Dora demands vote in Parliament!'

'Turn back!' she heard a man growl at her. Dora looked up to see a big policeman bar her way.

'Turn back,' he said again.

No fear! Not now, not when she was so near. Taking a deep breath Dora charged, swerving round the constable, half slipping in her clogs, but there was another of them behind him. Darting past him too, Dora laughed in his face. But she'd laughed too soon. One arm stretched out and seized her wrist. And struggle as she might, he was stronger than her.

The policeman looked down at the girl twisting and turning in his hand as if she was a fish on the end of a line. 'Eh, but you're just a child.'

He sounded astonished – as if he'd landed a minnow when he thought to have reeled in a big fat trout. 'What are you doing here? Sightseeing?'

Dora shook her arm. 'Get off me!'

'You should be home with your mother, a young 'un like you.' The policeman shook his head disapprovingly. 'I'd take a strap to you if you were one of mine.'

'I'm thankful I'm not one of yours then!' Dora retorted.

'You cheeky young thing! Will you go back?'

'Not till I've been in Holloway,' Dora shouted, pulling on his arm hard.

'Eh, Bill, give me a hand with this one, proper firebrand I've got here,' the constable called, holding Dora's arm in a vice-like grip. His fingers pinched deep into her arm. It hurt. But she wouldn't let him see how much.

A constable came up to seize Dora's other arm. Now they were trying to pinion them behind her back. She wouldn't let them.

'Will you go quietly,' said the constable again.

'Never,' she cried and pulled again at their arms, trying to shake them off. Her shawl had fallen down around her shoulders. She felt her hair slip loose.

The constable shook his head at her. 'You're a disgrace, you are. I'm arresting you, young lady.'

Dora laughed. She had done it. She had been arrested. How proud of her they would be at home. She would suffer in Holloway like the rest – she might be young, but she was as good as them, she'd shown them. She had won her battle spurs!

As Dora was hauled away, she saw one of the Lancashire mill girls struggling with another burly constable. The girl bent down and bit his hand. The policeman howled shaking his hand – what a baby! – and let her go. Off the mill hand scampered, slap into the arms of another constable. He was none too gentle with her, Dora thought indignantly, and now the first one was coming up red-faced. How long would she get for that?

'Take her into custody,' a voice yelled in Dora's ear.

'Well done, women. Rise up! Rise up!'

As she was marched away, Dora glimpsed two well-known faces smiling at her from a hansom cab. Mrs Pankhurst and Annie Kenney! Annie – the shawl of a mill hand over her head – raised her arm upwards. 'Rise up, women. Rise up!'

'Votes for women!' came back the cry from the women. Dora pulled and struggled. She wouldn't go quietly. Not she! Men and women lined the pavements, shouting and waving encouragement. Oh, how glorious it was! She was doing it for her mam and her sisters, for Mary. What would Mary think if she could see her now? She began to sing, 'Rise up women, for the fight is hard and long, rise in thousands, singing loud a battle song…'

A man slipped out of the crowd and Dora saw a camera flash full in her face. She blinked, turning her head aside and called out, 'Rise up women! Rise up I say!' Let those in the crowd hear her message. Let them all hear it. The camera flashed again. The spectators cheered. A man punched the air. Oh, it was marvellous! Life felt very good.

Handcuffs clipped on, Dora was bundled into a black

van. She swivelled around in her seat to look out of the window. A line of suffragettes was marching behind the van, just as she had marched behind arrested suffragettes earlier. As the van sped off across Parliament Square towards Cannon Row police station, the women began to run. Some of the crowd ran with them.

'Look at them!' a woman arrested with Dora said.

'The government has a fight on its hands,' said Dora. 'It's not just us, it's all people.'

'Enough, you,' said the constable firmly. Dora and the other woman looked at each other and laughed.

'You'll laugh on the other side of your faces down at the station,' the constable said grimly.

No, she wouldn't. She could face whatever they threw at her. She had done it. She had got herself arrested. And that was all that mattered.

Chapter Twenty-six

'Dear, dear me,' said Mr Horace Smith, peering in astonishment at the girl standing before him in the dock. 'I see you are only seventeen.

'Only sixteen,' Dora murmured to herself, staring resolutely back at the magistrate. She felt like laughing. It was a serious matter being brought into court on a charge of disorderly conduct and resisting the police – wasn't that what Chas Batterby, the arresting officer had said – but oh, he did look funny, that magistrate. As if she was the first young girl ever to come before him in court.

It was the morning after Dora's arrest. After a short ride to Cannon Row police station, she had been put in a cell with several others who had already been arrested. Sitting on the stone floor, they had sung songs and talked, joined one by one by arrested suffragettes until the cell was full to bursting. Mr Pethick-Lawrence had had his hands full bailing out the arrested suffragettes that evening and it was late by the time they learnt they could leave – on condition they appeared before the magistrate in court the following morning. And now here she was, number 46 to be tried, still in her mill dress, shawl draped over her head and shoulders.

'But you are only a child,' the magistrate spluttered. 'You don't know what you are doing!'

Dora laughed quietly. 'You are wrong, your honour,' she thought. 'I know exactly what I'm doing.'

'It is a great pity you should have been brought up here,' the magistrate said. 'Where do you come from?'

Dora cast her eyes down and said meekly, 'Huddersfield.'

'Who let you escape from Huddersfield?'

Dora looked the magistrate straight in the eye. 'A lot did!' A titter ran round the court room. Dora's eyes danced merrily and she turned round and smiled at the suffragettes crammed into the back of the court to watch proceedings. There were plenty of newsmen there too, she noted. Mrs How-Martyn and Mrs Despard, who had been looking after her in London, smiled back at her encouragingly.

'I don't know who pays the expenses of these poor women and girls.' It was that pompous lawyer speaking. What was his name again? Muskett?

Dora bridled. How dare he talk like that! Why, she had money of her own, hard-earned money.

Horace Smith shook his head. 'The child cannot be a delegate or anything else. She doesn't know what she is doing.' He turned to Dora and said angrily, 'You ought to be at school. It is really a shocking thing that you should be brought up to London to be turned loose on the London streets to come into collision with the police. It is disgraceful. Where is your mother?'

Dora's head went up. 'But I come for my mother and my sisters,' she said proudly. As if he cared about the fate of those poor girls and women who had no home but the London streets!

'But you ought to have come with your mother. It is shocking.' Another amused titter ran round the courtroom. The magistrate coughed.

'Will this poor child promise to go back? Though I don't think it is any good trying to help or reason with this class of woman. It is absolutely futile,' said Mr Muskett, shaking his head. Dora gave him a hard stare. The nerve of the man! There was no need for him to insult her like that. They didn't understand, neither of them did.

'I don't wish to go back, sir,' she said firmly. She'd come here to go to prison and to prison she would go. For too long women and girls like her had been invisible. But no longer.

'But you can't stay in London all your life,' said the magistrate.

'I shall remain here as long as the WSPU wants me,' Dora declared.

'I repeat, it is disgraceful,' said Mr Smith, 'and the matter ought to be taken notice of. It is disgraceful for everybody concerned. The child shall be remanded in custody till Wednesday and I shall communicate with her parents.'

He rapped on the desk. 'Next!' he said wearily.

He thinks I'm not a respectable girl, thought Dora furiously as she was taken down to the cells below. Men like him, they don't know anything about the lives of girls like me. School! That's a fine one! Doesn't he know that girls like me leave school at twelve to work full time in the mill! Begin work half-time when we are still children? But – oh joy! – she had achieved the aim she had set her heart on. She was going to prison for the cause – and she'd not be alone there either.

The night before she'd been overjoyed to discover that four of them from Huddersfield branch had been arrested. Ellen Brooke hadn't got as far as Old Palace Yard, but had been stopped earlier, at Parliament Square, and another of their number, Mrs Pinnance, had had the honour of leading the evening raid! Four out of the ten arrested. They may have been a small band, but they'd made up for it in spirit and determination and valour.

Chapter Twenty-seven

'Rise up women, for the fight is hard and long. Rise in thousands, singing loud a battle song,' the women sang as the Black Maria rattled over the cobblestones towards Holloway gaol. Dora poked her face up close to the iron grating in her tiny cage. With each bump of the van she felt as if every bone in her body was being picked up and shaken.

Each of the women sat in her own little cell in the van – 'It's as if they think we're wild animals to be tamed,' said one.

'Well, they've seen our claws, haven't they!' said another.

'Separate we may be, but not in spirit,' declared a third, stoutly.

She was right, thought Dora. They could put them in cages, hide them away in prison cells, but they couldn't stop their spirits from reaching out to each other – and to women everywhere.

The van sped through the gates of Holloway gaol. At the entrance was a pair of stone griffins, which stared balefully at the prisoners. On one of the gaol's foundation stones was inscribed the words, 'May God protect the City of London and make this place a terror to evil-doers.'

The van lurched to a stop, and the back was opened. One by one the tiny cells were unlocked and the women let down.

Close to, the soaring turrets of the prison made it look like a medieval fortress. Dora felt her heart thump. How long would she have to spend in such a fearsome place? she wondered as they were marshalled into line.

A wardress opened a prison ledger. 'Name. Age. Job. Address. Religion. Education,' they were asked in turn. Even their eye colour was recorded. Then they were marched into the prison.

'You're to come with me,' the wardress said to Dora once they were inside.

'But … I don't understand,' Dora's voice faltered. Why was she being separated from her comrades? She looked round at them. They looked as surprised as she was.

'Don't you fret,' one of them murmured, reaching out to give Dora's arm a comforting squeeze.

'Yours in the cause,' another said loudly.

'No talking,' the wardress's voice rapped.

Dora looked up at the wardress. No emotion showed on her face. It was as grim as the walls of the prison. There would be little use appealing to her.

'Follow me,' the wardress said. Bewildered, Dora followed the woman down the passage and into a room, where she was told to undress and bathe.

'Must I?' she asked. The wardress nodded.

'You must undress and take everything off. Including that,' she nodded at the locket Dora was wearing around her neck.

Dora's hand flew protectively to cover it. 'But it is years since I have taken my locket off,' she said.

'Nevertheless, you must take it off now.' Dora's hand struggled with the clasp, but her trembling fingers refused to undo it.

The wardress sighed impatiently. 'Let me,' she said, leaning forward.

Dora felt dry fingers briefly brush her neck. With a sudden yank the chain was off – and Dora looked down to see her beloved locket lying in two broken pieces on the ground. She put a hand to her neck. The rough gesture had hurt it. But she wouldn't let this horrible woman see how she felt.

She bent down to pick up the pieces but the wardress scooped them up first and said that she'd have the locket back when she was released.

The bath was old and dirty. Dora shuddered, dipping in a toe and hastily withdrawing it again. But at least the water was hot. When she got out, she was handed a pile of clothes.

'There must be a mistake,' Dora exclaimed. 'These are

not my clothes.' She looked at them in distaste. A horrid bulky serge gown, cap and apron with arrows on them. Coarse woollen stockings. Big clumpy boots that looked far too big for her.

'These are for you. Get dressed – and be quick about it.'

'Am I not to put my own clothes back on?' Dora protested. Surely she wasn't expected to wear prison clothes. She had not been given a sentence. She was still only on remand.

The wardress shook her head. 'No,' she said shortly, adding, 'Perhaps you won't come here again, if you wear these.' She shook her head as Dora reached for the cap. 'Wait. I must take down your hair first. I 'ave to check it.'

She pulled out the combs in Dora's hair, and ran her fingers through it. Dora tried not to shake the woman's hands away. What did she expect to find, she thought indignantly, as she put up her hair again. She treats me as if I am a common criminal. The wardress pocketed the combs. 'You'll 'ave these back when you're released,' she said.

Dora tied the strings of her cap under her chin. What must I look like, she wondered, looking down at herself. The gown was too big and her stockings were baggy and rumpled.

'Follow me, number 46.' Dora flinched. Number 46. It

was the number on the yellow disc on her prison gown. Was even her name to be taken from her in this dreadful place?

Down passage after long passage and row after row of silent cells Dora was marched, her feet echoing hollowly on the stone floors. Which of the cells held her friends and comrades? Dora wondered. When would she see them again? All the Huddersfield women had chosen to go to prison for fourteen days rather than pay a fine. Fourteen days! It was double the sentences that had been handed down to the suffragettes imprisoned in February. They are trying to make an example of us, Dora thought. Stop the demonstrations once and for all. She heard a baby cry and its mother's voice trying to hush it.

'Quiet! Number 85,' the wardress barked as they passed the cell. Were babies locked up in here? Dora thought, appalled. She tried to imagine what it must be like for a mother and child to be locked up in such a place as this. If they could bear it, then so could she, she told herself. Unlike them she had chosen to be here. She had come here, eyes open, and it was her duty to make the best of it. She was doing it for the cause. For Mam, for her sisters. Only – it was not quite what she had expected. The suffragettes had talked about their experiences of prison at meetings, and Miss Beever had tried to prepare her for it before they had left Huddersfield, but somehow what they had said had not sunk in. The excitement, the stirring words – that was what had led her to this place. Remembering those words now, Dora's head went up. I will write to my parents, she thought. I will tell them to make the magistrate give me the same sentence as the other women. It is only right. I must not let them down.

They stopped outside a cell. Number 46. Taking a key from the bunch she held in her hand, the wardress inserted it in the lock and turned it. The door grated over the stone floor as it swung open.

'This is your room, number 46,' the wardress said, beckoning to Dora. Dora walked in and stood there helplessly. What was going to happen now?

The door banged shut. The key turned in the lock. She was a prisoner – and alone. Dora tried to calm her mind. She saw a stool in one corner of the cell and sat down on it, resting her chin on her hands. After a few minutes she felt calmer. She got up and walked around. The cell was tiny. Four or five steps took her from one end to the other. Then as she walked back across the cell she saw something she hadn't noticed before – a peephole in the door. Behind it her wardress's face gazed in at her. Was she gloating over her predicament? Dora wondered. Resolutely, she turned her back on the door. She would not let that woman see how she felt. They would not break her resolve. Never, ever! But why, oh why, she thought disconsolately, as she heard the departing thump of the wardress's boots, had she been separated from every one of her suffragette comrades?

She turned back to inspect her cell. As well as the stool, there was a plank bed along one wall. A sort of shelf contained a tin mug and plate. Underneath the shelf was a rolled-up mattress and bedding, a pillow balanced on top. High up in the wall there was a small barred window. At least she would be able to look out then. Holding up the skirt of her gown in one hand, Dora clambered eagerly up on to the stool. Standing on tiptoe she could just see beyond the prison walls to the spire of a church. She climbed back down again and resumed her inspection of her cell.

There wasn't a lot more to see. Stone floor. Pipes that ran round the cell for warmth. She crouched down to touch them. They felt lukewarm. The cell was lit but she could not turn the light on or off from inside the cell. Her eyes scanned the walls. No clock. Her heart sank. How would she know what time it was? On one wall was pinned a list – regulations, no doubt. She would read them – but not now. Dora felt very tired suddenly. She had been too nervous and excited the night before to get much sleep. I must be brave, she told herself. I must be strong. It is for a good and noble cause that I am here. But if only she didn't feel so terribly alone. Dora sank down on the stool and put her arms round her head.

Chapter Twenty-eight

The harsh jangling of a bell jerked Dora out of her slumber. At first she could not think where she was. Then on came the light. Dora blinked and rubbed her eyes. She saw bare walls, a tiny window high up in the wall. Her heart sank. She was in prison – and it was the first full day of her imprisonment. Could it really be 5.30 already? she thought, wearily swinging her legs to the floor. They felt shaky as she stood up. It had been impossible to get a good night's rest on such a hard bed. At eight the previous night she had been startled to see the light go out. That had been the worst time. The deep darkness in that gloomy place had frightened her. She had shut her eyes tightly and tried to sleep. Tried not to think of her family, of Hawthorne Terrace. But almost as soon as she managed to drift off something had always woken her up again. The wail of a child, a warder's gruff command, the tramp of feet up and down the corridor.

Down the corridor now Dora could hear doors open and bang shut again. She must hurry to wash and dress before the wardress reached her cell. She rubbed a rag hastily over her face, then she put on the heavy serge dress, her fingers trembling as she tied the strings of her cap neatly under her chin. Her heavy woollen stockings kept falling down around her ankles. The horrid things! She heard the door next to hers bang shut. Now it was her turn. An eye peered in through the peephole. A key jangled in the lock. Slowly the heavy iron door rasped open.

'Empty your slops, number 46.'

Hateful task!

Then there was the bed to make and the floor to be scrubbed. Dora bent down to make her bed as she had been instructed. First, all the bedclothes had to be folded up into a roll like a giant sausage, then the utensils had to be polished till they shone using a bath brick and soap. Lastly the floor, chair and plank bed were to be scrubbed with a pail of water, which was brought in and dumped down at her feet by the wardress. And all before breakfast!

7.15. Tramp tramp tramp. Up and down. Doors opening and shutting. Nerves astrung, Dora heard steps come to a halt again outside her cell. She jumped up hastily, the floor half cleaned, the rag still in her hand. An eye pressed to the peephole again. She stared back defiantly.

The door swung open and the wardress clumped in. Dora swore her lip curled as she glanced at the half-cleaned floor.

'Hold out your pot, number 46,' she ordered. Dora

picked it up and held it out, shuddering as the gruel was slopped in. A piece of bread was plonked on her plate. The night before she'd been given cocoa to drink. It was cold and greasy and had nearly made her sick. The door banged shut. Dora took the fare to the shelf that served as her table and tried to eat. Her neck still hurt. She put a hand to it and felt it gingerly. It had been painful ever since the wardress had tugged off the locket yesterday. Had it really been only yesterday?

At 8.30 doors up and down the corridor were opened again and the inmates instructed to step outside and form a line with the other prisoners.

'Where are we going?' Dora whispered to the woman in front of her.

'Chapel,' the woman murmured.

'Silence, number 45, number 46,' rapped the wardress.

The woman's shoulders sagged slightly.

Down the corridor the prisoners were marched, up and down staircases and countless passages each the mirror of the one before. When they reached the chapel they were ordered to stop. Dora's spirits lifted a little. Now she would see her comrades again. What joy it would be to see a friendly face, maybe even exchange a few whispered words. But to her surprise she was taken right to the back of the chapel and told to stand behind a wooden barrier away from the other prisoners. All Dora could see of them were

154

the backs of hundreds of white-capped heads. So even here she was to be kept apart from her friends.

'You will stand here – baby suffragette,' a wardress said close to Dora's ear. Another wardress guffawed – as if it had been a funny thing to say.

How dare they call me a baby! Dora thought indignantly. The wardresses' eyes slid to each other and then to Dora. Dora caught the look. It had been said on purpose to taunt her. That was clear.

It had been only the beginning of the taunts. 'So you think you – a baby – should have the vote then?' her wardress said conversationally the next day. Dora didn't answer.

'I do it for others,' she muttered to herself. Others who have abandoned me, she thought bitterly. Not one visit had she had, not even a letter from home to comfort and encourage her. But worse than the taunts were the threats. 'Think you'll be out soon, do you?' the wardress said. 'Be warned. This is only the beginning. When your case comes up next week his honour will sentence you to a whole month.'

'That will learn you,' put in another. 'Teach you to think you can 'ave what you shouldn't 'ave.'

'Aye, wasting your time on a hopeless cause.'

'It isn't hopeless!' Dora had tried to keep her temper.

'Must be if they get children to fight it for them!'

She begged to be able to see her friends.

'Ladies like Mrs How-Martyn and the sister of General French are not fit friends for the likes of you,' the wardress replied contemptuously when she explained who they were.

The solitude weighed on Dora even more than the silence. The only voices she heard were the wardresses' and the priest's in chapel. Why were they so cruel to her? she thought bleakly, sitting on her stool and staring at the walls of the cell. What had she done to deserve such harsh treatment?

By Sunday, Dora felt she could not bear it any more. She felt tired and weak from the lack of proper food and sleep. And – oh – a horrible thought suddenly struck her. What if the wardress had been right? What if this was only the beginning of a much longer stretch in prison? And, her terrified mind ran on, what if her father had persuaded the magistrate to give her the same sentence as the other suffragettes? Another week in prison! Another whole week! How would she bear it! Dora slid down on to the floor and put her head in her hands and sobbed.

Lost to the world, she did not hear the wardress's steps outside the door, or see her lift up the flap to peer in. The wardress looked at the girl hunched up on the floor, her head in her hands. She nodded as if satisfied. The harsh medicine was working. That child would think twice before risking another stretch in prison. She looked at the two letters in her hand, and pondered. She might as well give them to her now, she decided at last. It would do no harm to remind her of home.

Dora looked up bleakly as the door grated open. What did they want of her now? 'Letters for you,' the wardress said, thrusting them inside. The door clanged shut, but not before the wardress had seen a faint smile light up the girl's tear-stained face.

'Dora looked at the envelopes lying on her lap. They had already been opened, she saw. But she felt too weary to care. There were two – both from her family.

'Dear child,' her mother had written. 'I am very proud of you and the way you have acted, so keep your spirits up and be cheerful. And do your duty by the WSPU.'

Dora laid her head down on her arms again and wept. It was too much. How could she do what they expected of her? They didn't know how badly she was being treated.

Wiping her eyes on her sleeve, she opened the other envelope.

'We all miss you,' she read. 'We feel so lonely without you. George does not like the idea of your going to prison. He says you see no danger in anything. Cheer up!'

And how I miss you, she thought plaintively. Her merry sisters, the little ones. Mam and Dad. Why, oh, why had she left them? Dora choked back her tears as she put the letters back in their envelopes. She sat still, the letters clutched in her hand, thinking. There were only two days to go before her case would be brought up again. It wasn't long, but … but what if this was only the beginning? How did the prisoners bear it? Dora had seen some of them cry in chapel – a sad hymn, or some thoughtful words from the priest, and their tears began to flow. What crimes could such poor broken-down women possibly have committed? she found herself wondering. Woman's lot was indeed a hard one. Dora's heart swelled at the injustice of it all. Yes, they were right to demand the vote. So much was wrong, so much needed putting right. But if only she could go home …

Chapter Twenty-nine

The door clanged open. Huddled on her stool, Dora looked up wanly. The wardress smiled. She could see that the girl's spirit was breaking. She looked pale and listless. She would let her see her visitor, who had been most importunate. 'You have a visitor, number 46.'

Dora stood up shakily, her weakness and weariness almost forgotten. Who could it be? she wondered. Surely it was too much to hope that they had relented and were allowing her to see one of her suffragette comrades.

'Follow me, number 46,' came the monotonous words. She was led down the corridor and shown into the reception cell. As the door shut behind her a man stood up. Dora looked at him in surprise. Why, he was a stranger? But after several days in prison any friendly face was a welcome relief.

'Oh, I am so glad to see you,' she cried, impulsively. 'I am so lonely here. I wish I could go home. No one has been to see me. It is too bad.' Her voice quivered. 'My only comfort has been two letters I have had from home.'

The man looked at her sympathetically. He had last

seen her in the courthouse and had been impressed by the spirited answers she had given the magistrate. But he could scarcely believe this was the same girl. She looked pale and thin.

He cleared his throat. 'Miss Thewlis, I am a journalist,' he said. 'I witnessed your bold fight outside Parliament last week. My readers would like to know how you have been treated in prison.' He looked at her expectantly. The girl looked startled, he thought. Didn't she know that her picture had been splashed all over the papers? Or what a stir it had caused? Everyone had wanted to know who she was.

As he explained Dora grew even more bewildered. How had a reporter managed to wheedle his way into prison to see her? And what was he talking about? Her picture – in the newspapers? But at least he was someone to talk to – and as her wardress was outside the room she was free to say whatever she liked.

'The food is awful,' she burst out. 'I have eaten practically nothing since I got here. And look at me.' She stared down at herself in disgust. 'These awful clothes. They are too big and heavy. They tire me.' The words poured out. 'At present my family are very proud of me, but I do not think they will be tomorrow, for I intend asking the magistrate to let me go home. I am too tired and ill to stay here,' she said brokenly. She had a defeated look, the reporter thought. That young girl suffragette whose black dancing eyes and ready answers to the magistrate in the courtroom had entranced his readers looked sad and ill, as if prison had beaten her down. But then a flash of Dora's old spirit seemed to return. 'I will carry on the fight,' she told the reporter determinedly. 'But at home, not in London – not unless they let us enter the House of Commons like ladies.'

The reporter was grim-faced as he left. That girl had been treated badly, her resolve deliberately broken. He knew that working-class girls like Dora endured a harsher time in prison than the well-to-do. 'The warders taunt me,' she had told him. 'They say what do I want with the vote? That I am too young to vote. But it is not for myself that I have been fighting.' What a story for his readers!

As Dora was led back to her solitary cell, she pondered. The reporter's ready sympathy and eagerness to listen to whatever she had to tell him had helped to lift her spirits. And – whatever happened in court tomorrow – it seemed as if her actions had at least achieved some publicity for the cause.

Chapter Thirty

The magistrate looked up at the wan-faced girl who had been hurried into the dock. It was the Wednesday following Dora's first court appearance.

'I understand that you wish to go home,' he said drily.

'Yes sir, yes sir,' Dora answered eagerly.

'Very well, I will make arrangements for you to return home,' he said. 'Case dismissed.'

Sitting at the back of the court amongst the spectators Mrs How-Martyn and Mrs Despard were shocked by the change they saw in Dora. She looked pale and listless – as if all the fight had been drained out of her.

'The girl has clearly been starved into submission,' said Mrs How-Martyn angrily. And as soon as Dora had left the courtroom, the women rose from their seats. 'We must find her and speak to her,' Mrs How-Martyn said.

Outside the courtroom she hailed an official. 'I am sorry – we cannot allow you to see or speak to Miss Thewlis,' the official said in answer to their request.

The two women looked at each other. 'But we must see her. We are responsible to Mrs Thewlis for her daughter's safety,' said Mrs How-Martyn.

The official shook his head. 'You may not see her.'

'Very well,' said Mrs How-Martyn angrily. She scribbled a note and handed it to the official. 'Please make sure that the magistrate receives this.' She gave him a tight-lipped nod.

'Of a certainty he will not answer it,' said Mrs Despard as they stood and conferred in the hall. Mrs How-Martyn agreed. All their previous requests to visit Dora in prison had been refused, and they had no reason to think that the magistrate would change his mind now. They made their way out of the courthouse into the street.

'Where now?' said Mrs Despard.

'To the station,' Mrs How-Martyn decreed. 'They are bound to take her straight there. Cab,' she called, holding out her umbrella.

A four-wheeler drove up to the pavement.

'Where to?' asked the driver, hopping down and opening the door for them.

'King's Cross station,' said Mrs How-Martyn as the two women climbed inside.

The suffragettes had not been the only spectators to learn of Dora's release from prison. Sitting in court was a battalion of eager journalists and photographers. As soon as Dora had left the courtroom they too had hurried out after her, eager to interview the girl. But there was no sign of her. The reporters rushed out into the street – but Dora had gone.

Dora closed her eyes and leant back in her seat. Seeing a flurry of eager reporters outside the court, the wardress appointed to escort Dora home had hurried the girl out of a back entrance and into a waiting cab. She told the cabbie to take the shortest route to the station.

'What train do you want to catch?' the driver had asked.

'The 1.30,' the wardress answered.

The driver sighed and raised his whip. They were always in a hurry. 'How the 'eck do they think they'll catch that train,' he grumbled to himself. 'Don't they know about London traffic?'

He too had seen the reporters as they had driven away from the courthouse and he had caught sight of his passenger as she'd climbed into the cab. Blimey, he thought. It's 'er. The baby suffragette. He had seen her picture in the papers. But there was nothing he could do about that traffic. He slumped back in his seat as the horse slowed to an amble.

The cab crawled along the street. Oh, hurry, hurry, Dora thought. I want to go home. On her head was a motoring cap, which had been bought for her earlier by the elderly wardress. The indignity of it. 'My hat and coat,' Dora had explained. 'I left them at the' – she hesitated – 'at the WSPU's offices in Clement's Inn. Might I not get them?'

'No,' said the wardress firmly. 'I will buy you a hat, using money out of the poor box.'

Dora flushed. It was another indignity. 'I will pay for it. I have money of my own,' she said proudly, 'which I have saved out of my wages.' But the wardress had refused. It was too bad of her, Dora thought. Nor had they let her speak to her suffragette comrades. Dora had seen Mrs How-Martyn and Mrs Despard among the suffragettes sitting at the back of the court. She had been pleased to see them there – and relieved to find that she had not been forgotten as she had feared. But she had not even been allowed to greet them. And to add to the insults and indignities she had already suffered at the hands of the authorities, her train fare was being paid out of the poor box too.

How different this journey was to the one she had undertaken a week earlier. How full of hope she had been then. As the cab jolted across the square Dora looked out of the window. She could see the House of Commons, the great Parliament building they had tried to enter a week ago. Only a week ago. Was it possible? The sight of it now mocked her. They had failed in their aim. They had failed to get Parliament to give them the vote. Had it been worth it? She felt no trace now of the excitement she had felt that day, only weariness and a deep longing to be at home.

As the cabbie had predicted, they missed their train. A full half-hour they'd have to wait for the next one. And that was a slow one, too. Grumbling to herself, the wardress went off to buy their tickets. She ordered Dora to stay where she was. 'Don't speak to the press now,' she said.

She'd seen the men hovering around, cameras and notebooks in hand. She shook her fist at them. 'The cads!' she muttered to herself. 'Be off with you.'

As soon as the wardress had gone two figures who had kept quietly in the background rushed up to Dora: Mrs How-Martyn and Mrs Despard.

'Oh, I am so pleased to see you,' cried Dora, taking their outstretched hands in hers. Then she felt confused. What must they think of her, begging the magistrate to let her go home!

Mrs How-Martyn looked with concern at Dora's pale face. 'We were worried about you,' she said. 'We tried to visit you in prison, but the magistrate would not allow us to. Rest assured, we will write to him to remonstrate about your treatment.'

'I am glad to be going home,' Dora said simply. She lowered her eyes. 'I am sorry that I did not stay in prison longer,' she said. 'But I feel so ill.'

Mrs How-Martyn patted her hand. 'You did all that could be expected of you,' she said kindly. The tall figure of the wardress bore down on them. She glared at the two women.

'I had better go now,' Dora said and bid them a hasty farewell. She climbed on to the train and sat down next to the wardress in a third-class compartment. From her seat near the window she could see Mrs How-Martyn and Mrs Despard still standing on the platform. Mrs How-Martyn looked up and caught Dora's eye. She smiled. It was too much. The memories came flooding back.

Dora ran to the train door and snatched a kiss. 'Goodbye,' she cried. 'Goodbye.'

The guard blew his whistle and waved his flag. The train began to move out of the station. Dora still stood at the door, her eyes fixed on the two suffragettes, watching as they grew smaller and smaller.

Dora's mother paced up and down the station platform anxiously. It was nearly half past seven. The train was late. But would Dora even be on it? she wondered. The Thewlises had been waiting at Huddersfield railway station for over half an hour. They had been told to expect her on an earlier train. The train had arrived, but Dora had not been on it.

'It's coming, Mam,' called Evie suddenly. 'I can hear it!'

Evie and Flo looked at each other. They felt nervous suddenly. They had read Dora's story in the paper and were worried about her. Their sister had lots of pluck. She must indeed have been badly treated in prison to ask the magistrate to let her go home. They were proud of her too. She had carried the fight to Parliament as she had said she would and had gone to prison for the cause. The train emerged from the tunnel into the station. Steam swirled around the girls as they ran up and down the platform, gazing up at the windows of the train, searching for their sister's face. Passengers began to descend from the train. Where was Dora? Had she missed this train too? 'There she is, Mam!' Mabel cried at last, pointing a finger at one of the windows where a girl was waving eagerly. The girls ran up to the carriage door.

There they were, thought Dora happily. Mam and three of her sisters. She jumped down eagerly and ran up to them. The sisters threw their arms around each other. How comforting it was to feel their warm arms around her, Dora thought. How she had missed them all. Now she hoped she could put it all behind her – all the events of the past week.

Even on the train Dora had been accosted by passengers anxious to talk to the young suffragette. All of them it seemed had seen her photograph in the newspaper. That wretched photograph. Was it always to haunt her, even here, at home? Dora thought wearily, seeing some of the people on the platform stare and whisper among themselves.

'Will you carry on the fight, Miss Thewlis?' some of the passengers had asked inquisitively.

'It's for others to do that now,' Dora had replied. 'I've had enough.' And it was true. She had had enough – for now.

One of the men standing on the platform detached himself from a group and went up to the family. 'Excuse me, Miss Thewlis. I wonder if you would give me a few words?'

Reluctantly Dora disentangled herself from her sisters. She put up a hand. 'You mustn't speak to me. I shan't say anything,' she said quickly.

The wardress walked up to the reporter. 'You are a newspaper man, I suppose?' she said, folding her arms.

'I am,' the man owned. 'I'd like a short interview with Miss Thewlis.'

'Miss Thewlis has nothing to say to you,' the wardress said firmly.

The reporter's eyebrows went up. Indeed. 'And who might you be?' he said, looking the wardress up and down. An elderly suffragette, he supposed, and a right old battleaxe too.

The wardress drew herself up and fixed him with

her eye. 'I was sent down here with her by the London magistrate.'

'Well, we're out of his patch here,' said the reporter smoothly. He whipped his notebook out of his pocket and sauntered back to the family. 'Miss Thewlis,' he called. 'Haven't you anything to say? You can say what you like here, you don't have to worry about her.' He jerked his head at the wardress.

Dora shook her head. The reporter chewed his pencil thoughtfully. His boss wanted a story and a story he would have. Tomorrow he would try again.

'Aren't you going to tell us about it?' Flo asked eagerly, as the reporter strolled away. 'All your adventures? The raid on Parliament. Prison.'

Evie glared at Flo. How could she be so thoughtless? 'Shut up!' she hissed.

Dora looked away. The sun was sinking, she saw. In Holloway gaol now they would be turning off the lights soon. Only last night she had been lying in that cell, on her hard wooden bed. She shivered at the memory. 'Not now,' she said. 'I don't want to talk about it now.'

But there was something that she did need to talk about. Best do it now. Get it over with. 'Are you angry with me, Mam – for asking to come home?' Dora said in a low voice to her mother. 'For not taking the fight further than I did. I wanted so much for you all to be proud of me. But

I couldn't stay in prison. I felt so ill.' She put up her hand to her neck. It still hurt. 'They taunted me. They broke my locket.' Her voice broke.

'I am proud of you. We all are,' said her mother quietly. 'As for how they treated you, your father will be writing to the authorities about it.'

Weariness was making Dora's every limb ache. She felt as if she could sleep for a year. 'Can we go home now, Mam?' she pleaded. 'I am so tired.' She draped her arms over her sisters' shoulders.

'Come on, you girls,' she said, 'aren't you going to help your little sister home?'

Chapter Thirty-one

The reporter looked up at Dora expectantly. He was pleased that she had agreed to an interview. She looked tired and ill as she told him about her prison ordeal.

'I can see it more clearly now,' she said. 'By treating me like a criminal they hoped to break my spirit. They called me "child" and "a baby".'

She flushed at the memory. Pressing her hands together in her lap she went on. 'It made me see how futile it was to carry on the struggle. But…' Her black eyes flashed. 'I shall carry on the fight as long as I am able.' She looked full in the reporter's face and said pleadingly. 'But don't call me the "baby suffragette". I am not a baby. Not really. In May next year I shall be eighteen. Surely that is a good age for a girl?'

'Yes, all this talk of Dora being a baby is nonsense,' her mother broke in abruptly. 'She may be a baby compared to the other women, but she is as determined as me to carry on the fight for the cause. When she is eighteen my daughter will go again to London to assist in the raids on the House of Commons. And if necessary, she will go back to prison. If need be we will all go to prison for the cause,' she declared. 'But we insist on fair and just treatment. My husband is going to take every possible step to get an explanation from the government for Dora's treatment in Holloway.'

Dora leaned forward. 'I'm ready to go back to London now,' she declared. 'I did not carry the fight far enough.'

'That's enough, Dora,' said her father sharply.

Dora subsided. The episode was over to her father's mind. He didn't want to hear any more about it. The magistrate had made it clear that Dora would get a longer gaol term if she was arrested again.

The journalist got up to go. Dora accompanied him to the door. 'I have a message for you,' she whispered. The journalist looked at her, pencil poised over his notebook. 'I say, more women arise. Votes for women.' She heaved a deep sigh. 'I am going back in now. But only until I have got my strength back.' She gave him a smile in which there was a trace of the old fire. 'Next time we shall need as many women as there are helmets against us.'

'Was it worth it, Dora?' said Mary. The two girls were sitting together in the mill yard. Since returning to Huddersfield, Dora had talked and talked about her experiences but there were some things Mary still wanted to know. 'What will you do now? Will you carry on the fight?'

Dora stared past her friend. Had it been worth it? What would she do now? Would she carry on the fight?

All the women who had been imprisoned with her had now returned home. There was to be a big meeting in Huddersfield at which all the imprisoned suffragettes would sit on the platform – Dora amongst them – applauded as martyrs to the cause. But after that? I don't know, she thought. I don't know. She'd often thought about that day in London – the attempted raid on Parliament, the harsh treatment she had received in Holloway gaol. She still smarted from her treatment in prison. Had it been worth it? Mrs Key thought it had. She had told the press that she was proud of the Huddersfield women who had done and dared for the cause.

Since returning home Dora had pored over the papers. In spite of all they had done – 76 women arrested! – they were no nearer getting the vote. She had heard all about Lady Harberton's attempt to hand the resolution to the Prime Minister. Lady Harberton had succeeded in escaping the police and had actually got into the Lobby. But that was as far as she had got. She had not been allowed to hand the resolution to the Prime Minister, and her request to see him had been refused. Then there was all the attention she, Dora, had received. Eliza had received letters from important suffragettes congratulating her on her daughter's stand for the cause. There had been other letters too that Dora did not want to think about. Then the press clamouring at the door, people staring at her in the street. Everyone wanted to talk to her now they'd seen her picture plastered all over the papers. And she didn't like all they had to say either. She wanted to put that behind her now.

Was that all? No. There was something more. The suffragettes had shown her that women could take charge of their destiny.

'By joining the WSPU I was free to make my own choices,' Annie Kenney had told her. 'And I did.' Women could choose how they lived their lives. They did not have to abide by laws in the making of which they had no voice.

Dora looked up at the mills that surrounded the town. At the grimy terraces and streets, the windswept moors. At the tower on Castle Hill, where long ago the Chartists had spoken to the people in the early days of the great struggle for the vote. She too could choose her own destiny, couldn't she? What was it to be? Anything was possible – so long as you had courage.

Mary looked at her friend. She seemed very far away. Where was she, in spirit, now?

'I might go away,' Dora said suddenly.

'Away? Where?' Mary exclaimed.

Dora smiled. 'Far away,' she said. 'Australia, mebbe.' In nearly all Australian states women had been granted the vote. And the other states would be bound to follow. If women didn't get the vote in Britain, that was where she'd go. Aye, a girl could begin a new life in a young country like that.

'Australia! That's a way to go.'

The buzzer was sounding. Time for work.

'We'd best get back,' Dora said, getting up and smoothing down her skirts.

'Aren't you going to explain?' said Mary, clambering to her feet after her. She had something in her pocket she'd been wondering about showing Dora. It was a picture postcard of her. They were being sold in the shops. On it Dora was described as a 'Lancashire lass.' But it was unmistakably her. Mary wasn't sure she'd show it to her now. Another time, maybe.

'Come on, Mary,' Dora called back over her shoulder. 'Stop dallying, won't you, or Big Arthur will have words to say.'

Author's Note

When I first saw the picture postcard of a young suffragette outside Parliament, her arms in the firm grip of two burly policemen, I was intrigued. Who was she? I wondered. How did such a young girl come to be a suffragette? And then I discovered a book called *Rebel Girls*, by Jill Liddington. The suffragette's name I learned was Dora Thewlis, and she was a sixteen-year-old weaver from Huddersfield. And it was thanks to Jill Liddington's ground-breaking research that I learned a lot more about young Dora Thewlis. And I realized she would make a wonderful heroine in a book for young readers. But there was still much that I didn't know. Who of Dora's large family was living in the Hawthorne Terrace house in Huddersfield that was Dora's home at the time? What was the name of the mill where she worked? How involved was she in the Huddersfield branch of the WSPU before taking part in the great demonstration outside Parliament in March 1907?

In the effort to find answers to these and other questions, I trawled contemporary national and local newspapers, visited Huddersfield, hunted through books,

Huddersfield WSPU branch records, studied censuses (a record of everyone who lives in Britain that is taken every ten years), and investigated other historical sources. The interest shown by the press in Dora following her court appearance and subsequent imprisonment was invaluable. Some of Dora's grandchildren generously shared their memories of their grandmother, but she seems to have talked very little about her time as a suffragette, perhaps understandably wishing to put it behind her.

From one of Dora's grandchildren I was not surprised to learn that Dora was strong-willed and feisty – a woman who had true 'fire in her belly'. But details of her everyday life remained tantalizingly out of reach. Working-class women and girls were practically invisible in what was, in the late 19th and early 20th century, still very much a man's world. Finally I was thrown back on my imagination to fill in the gaps and to try and bring Dora's story alive in what I hope is a convincing way that honours the extraordinary accomplishments of Dora and the real-life characters that populate her story.

We will probably never know the whole truth of Dora's involvement with the suffragette movement in 1906–7 but there is one thing we can be sure of: Dora's courage and commitment, which took her to London and then to prison for the cause. We should be proud of women and girls like Dora. Their courage and bravery are an inspiration to us.

And we can do their memory no better service than by casting a vote at election time, remembering what they went through to get it for us.

Historical Note

I have already said, in my Author's Note, that there is much we do not know about Dora's young life. To give you a clearer idea of what is true and what is an author's invention, below is a little bit more about Dora and the principal people, places and events in the book.

The Thewlis Family

Dora was born in Honley, near Huddersfield, West Yorkshire in 1890, one of several children born to James and Eliza Thewlis. At the time of Dora's birth James was working locally as a weaver. The work was not well paid and Eliza and her eldest daughter also had to work in the mill. By the time Dora was aged about ten she too would have had to go out to work. Until she was about twelve she would have worked half time in the mill and spent the rest of the working day at school. But at twelve Dora's education would have ended, and like many other girls at that time she would have joined her elder siblings, working full time in the mill.

The Thewlises did not live in one house throughout Dora's childhood and teenage years. Like many other low-paid mill workers, they needed to move house quite frequently, while they tried to find better paid work to support their growing family. Most of this time they remained in West Yorkshire, but they also lived briefly in Lancashire when Dora was still at school.

By 1906, the Thewlis family were living at 29 Hawthorne Terrace – a street of small terraced houses in north Huddersfield that is still standing today. By this time most of the children were grown up and working full time, so it is probable that Eliza Thewlis would have been able to give up work. Her husband James ('Jim') still worked as a wool weaver. The 1911 census records that he was a fancy worsteds weaver, and it is likely that he was doing this work in 1906–7.

There are no census records for the years 1906 or 1907, but records of the Huddersfield WSPU branch show that at this time Dora was living at home. The youngest children – including Mabel and probably Arthur – would also have been living at home, but we do not know which, if any, of Dora's four elder sisters – Mary, Amy, Flora and Evelyn – still lived at Hawthorne Terrace. We know that Dora also had a brother called William, or Bill, who went to fight in South Africa.

George Taylor

George Taylor did exist. All I know about him is that he was Dora's sister's 'young man'. But which sister this was I do not know.

Mary

Dora's friend Mary is a fictional character. But there must have been girls like her, who shared Dora's enthusiasm for the cause, who were hampered by lack of support from their family.

The Mill

Dora was working full time as a wool weaver in 1906–7. Contemporary maps show that Huddersfield and its environs were dotted with wool and cotton manufacturing mills. We do not know which of them Dora and her family worked in but it is probable that Dora found work quite near where she lived. It seems that the woollen trade was thriving at this time, so to some extent weavers might have been able to pick and choose where they worked. However, the trade could easily slump so life for a family of weavers like Dora's would always have been unpredictable. There was little social protection for those out of work or unemployed. Those who had no family to care for them would have been forced to go to the dreaded workhouse, which still existed in Dora's day.

The mill processes I describe were typical of a woollen mill at the time. The room where weavers worked was known as a weaving 'shed'. The 'tuner' made sure that the looms were working properly, but Big Arthur, the tuner in my book is my invented character.

WSPU, Huddersfield Branch

The Huddersfield branch was founded in early 1907, one of the earliest branches of the WSPU to be set up by the Pankhursts. Most unusually, the branch's minute book for the time still exists, with its activities carefully recorded by Edith Key, the branch secretary. There is also a list of the early members so that we know who they were and where they lived. None of Dora's sisters are recorded as joining the branch, but Edith Key, Elizabeth Pinnance, Ellen Beever, Annie Sykes, Bertha Lowenthal and Ellen Brooke were all members of Huddersfield branch. Edith Key lived very near the Thewlises, in a house in Regent Place, off Bradford Road, where her blind husband kept a music shop. The house, at 68 Regent Place, still exists. The railway runs behind the house, so it would have been very noisy. Several other WSPU members lived in Huddersfield itself but a good number lived in villages outside the town. Elizabeth Pinnance, who lived in Paddock, led the demonstration on the evening of 20 March and was imprisoned along with Dora, who had been arrested earlier in Old Palace Yard.

Most members of the Huddersfield WSPU branch were poor. Only one of the early members of the branch, Bertha Lowenthal, came from a better-off family. Many – like the Thewlises – would also have been members of the Independent Labour Party, one of whose founder members ,– the MP Keir Hardie – went on to help found the modern Labour Party and was a staunch supporter of women's right to vote.

Did Dora chalk suffragette slogans on the pavement, or hand out leaflets to passers-by? We do not know. But these were activities that would have been taken on by branch members, so while Dora's job would have prevented her from taking a full role in the branch, it is quite probable that she helped out in this way. Her mother, Eliza Thewlis, claimed to a journalist that she and Dora were the first people to help Mrs Pankhurst in the Huddersfield by-election in November 1906 and while some of Eliza's claims, for instance that she was elected president of the local branch, are not noted in branch records, it is certain that she was a gifted speaker and an enthusiastic worker for the branch, frequently chairing and speaking at meetings, and it is likely that it was at this time that the Thewlises became active supporters of the new movement. Dora herself later told a journalist that she had been one of the main workers at the Huddersfield branch since she was thirteen – in 1903, the year the WSPU was set up. The

Huddersfield branch wasn't founded until early 1907, when Dora was sixteen, but maybe Dora meant that she had followed the activities of the WSPU from its beginnings, or even that she was involved in local Labour politics from that time. What we do know for certain is that Dora was brought up by staunchly socialist and progressive parents, both of whom supported the women's cause. I learnt from one of Dora's grandsons, Dora was passionately interested in politics all her life and was a lifelong supporter of the Labour Party.

The members' efforts, at this early period of the branch's existence, would probably have been taken up largely with plans for the WSPU's national campaigns – the big deputations to Parliament in February and March 1907. The big meetings at the Friendly and Trades Club and at Huddersfield's imposing Town Hall did take place, as did the meeting in Robinson's Cafe, when Mrs Pankhurst explained to the new members the organization's constitution and objectives, and the earlier procession across town following the release of the suffragettes from Holloway gaol though we do not know if Dora joined the march. Newspapers reports cover the meetings in the Town Hall and the Friendly and Trades Club thoroughly so we know who the speakers were and even many of their actual words. These are the only meetings I write about that I know did take place. The meetings of suffragettes at the Thewlises' house, and the gathering of suffragettes at Edith Key's house on the night of the February 1907 demonstration, are imaginary, although meetings at members' houses did take place during this year.

How much opposition was there to the new branch in its early days? It is hard to be sure. Opposition to the suffragettes locally does seem to have increased following the demonstrations outside Parliament in 1907 and we know that at an open-air meeting in nearby Marsden in the summer of 1907, Dora's mother and other local suffragettes were heckled and pelted with rotten eggs and forced to seek refuge at a fellow suffragette's home. Branch records also hint at disturbances at branch meetings.

The Suffragettes

All the leading suffragettes I mention in the book did exist, and important facts – for instance how Annie Kenney became a suffragette – are true, but I have had to draw on my imagination for my accounts of Dora's meetings with the suffragettes. Dora must have met Mrs Pankhurst when she first came up to speak in Huddersfield, in November 1906, and Annie Kenney and Adela Pankhurst – the youngest of Mrs Pankhurst's daughters – either then or soon afterwards. Adela Pankhurst and Annie Kenney played a significant role in the Huddersfield campaigns of 1906–7 as well as drumming up support for the new branch and for the February and March 1907 demonstrations in London.

Annie did arrange for Lancashire factory women to take part in the March demonstration and she wrote later in her memoir that no deputation to Parliament had given her as much satisfaction as this one did. It is also likely that Dora met other important suffragettes like Mary Gawthorpe and Mrs Mitchell, who were both working for the WSPU in the north at that time.

Mrs How-Martyn and Mrs Despard were also prominent members of the WSPU. They were apparently responsible for Dora whilst she was in London, and they attended Dora's appearances in court and were forbidden to visit Dora in prison or to make contact with her in the courthouse after her release. But – as newspaper accounts reveal – they did manage to catch up with Dora at King's Cross station before she was whisked away by the wardress who accompanied her home. Later in the year, unhappy at the increasing militancy of the WSPU, both women were to leave the WSPU to form a rival suffrage organization, the Women's Freedom League.

The Women's Parliament and March to the House of Commons, 20 March 1907

Journalists followed the suffragettes' activities avidly, and so there are any number of detailed articles in the contemporary press about the 20 March 1907 Women's Parliament in Caxton Hall and suffragette march to Parliament. And thanks to press interest in Dora, we know that she was arrested in the late afternoon in Old Palace Yard, outside the House of Commons. Journalists reported on both of Dora's court appearances, her time in prison and her journey home, they also interviewed her back in Hawthorne Terrace. Dora's parents were also interviewed by the press. Dora and her mother complained to the press about Dora's treatment in prison. Working-class women and girls seem to have been treated more harshly in prison than better-connected prisoners. In this respect suffragettes' vocal and written criticisms of the treatment of women in prison do seem to have helped improve conditions for women prisoners.

What Next?

After all the suffragette prisoners had been released in spring 1907, there was a meeting at which the ten Huddersfield 'martyrs' to the cause were present. After this Dora seems to slip from the suffragette picture. Maybe all the press attention and the subsequent publication of a picture postcard showing her demonstrating outside the House of Commons was too much for the teenager to cope with. Her parents might well have been warned by the London magistrate that Dora would face a longer spell in prison if she took part in another suffragette demonstration. Later that summer her mother was reproved officially by the branch for overbearing behaviour and she seems also to have disappeared from local suffrage activity.

What next? By her twentieth birthday Dora had moved into lodgings with her sister Evelyn in central Huddersfield. The 1911 census records both girls were still working as weavers in a woollen mill. It was to be only the first step in the girls' search for independence and a better life. In Britain women still had not won the right to vote, and some time before 1914 the two sisters took the giant step of emigrating to Australia along with a number of other Huddersfield girls. There Dora found work as a blanket weaver near Melbourne, married Australian Jack Dow, had two children and settled down happily in her new country.

A Brief History of the Women's Suffrage Campaign in Britain

By the end of the 19th century, women in a number of countries had gained the right to vote, but in Britain, in the early 20th century, women still did not have that right. By then most men in Britain could vote, following social upheavals and protests which led eventually to the great reform acts of the 19th century. Though some women had gained the right to vote at local council elections, few people in Britain thought that women were mentally equipped to vote for a member of Parliament. Women were all too often still viewed as emotionally unstable, fragile creatures, who lacked the mental capacity for serious thought. The idea that they should have the right to vote in a parliamentary election was viewed by most contemporaries as preposterous.

In the 19th and early 20th centuries even wealthy women had few rights, and limited life choices. Many professions were still closed to them. For the poor the only choices were lowly paid work and marriage. But not all women were satisfied with their lot. They wanted to have the same rights and opportunities as men.

During the 19th century poor and middle-class men had slowly begun to make headway in their campaign for the vote – which until then had been the preserve only of wealthy men – a few women's voices had risen, too, demanding that same right. Until they had the vote, women argued, they would never have true equality with men. And women like Emmeline Pankhurst, shocked by the conditions they witnessed in the workhouses, became convinced that it was only when women got the vote that their lives would improve. Gradually, women banded together to form 'suffrage' societies. The members of these societies were known as 'suffragists', which meant that they were women who sought the right to vote. Then in 1897 these societies became grouped together under one banner – that of the NUWSS (National Union of Women's Suffrage Societies), led by Millicent Fawcett. The mainly Liberal-supporting NUWSS stuck to peaceful means of pressing government for the right to vote – lobbying MPs, writing letters and petitions and holding rallies.

In 1903, frustrated by the NUWSS's lack of progress, Emmeline Pankhurst founded the WSPU (Women's Social and Political Union). Their approach would be different, radical, their motto 'deeds, not words'. All three of Emmeline's daughters – Christabel, Sylvia and Adela – became involved in the new organization. What must people have thought when the members of the WSPU first began to speak in public? Respectable women in Edwardian times did not climb on to wagons to speak to the crowds in public squares and other public places. These women were very brave and determined. They must have endured much heckling and abuse from those they attempted to address.

But it was in 1905 that the WSPU showed the British nation what they truly meant by 'deeds not words'. In October that year Christabel Pankhurst and Annie Kenney (the only working-class woman to become one of the WSPU's leaders) were imprisoned for disrupting a Liberal Party meeting in Manchester's Free Trade Hall. Ejected from the hall, Christabel allegedly spat at a policeman. Charged with obstruction and assault, the two women were given a choice: pay a fine or go to prison. The women chose prison. It was the first of many 'militant' acts by the WSPU. The women's imprisonment electrified the nation and more recruits joined the fledgling organization. Later Emmeline Pankhurst would write that it was the beginning of a campaign 'the like of which had never been seen before in England.'

The WSPU leadership, which had its beginnings in the Pankhursts' Manchester home, now moved to London, setting up office in Clement's Inn, where the WSPU was to become a highly efficient and well funded campaigning organization, with paid organizers responsible for different regions. Local branches sprang up across the nation. Working-class members were welcomed along with the well-to-do. Members flung themselves into a militant campaign, which included opposing electoral candidates of the sitting Liberal government, heckling speakers at meetings, and holding great demonstrations and noisy protests outside the House of Commons – with the aim of gaining press attention and keeping the cause alive in the public's mind. Then in 1906 the *Daily Mail* bestowed on members of the WSPU the name 'suffragette'. Though intended as an insult the name was proudly adopted by the WSPU.

As part of their campaign to keep the cause in the public eye, more women got themselves sent to prison. Not all suffragettes were happy with the militant methods adopted by the WSPU, however, and a number of prominent suffragettes left the organization to form other suffrage groups. Others objected to what they saw as Emmeline and Christabel Pankhurst's autocratic style of leadership.

In 1908 the suffragettes adopted the colours white (for

purity), purple (for dignity) and green (for hope) which were worn as sashes and emblems or carried as flags and banners at rallies and on demonstrations. Then in autumn 1908 Herbert Asquith was appointed Prime Minister. Asquith – a Liberal – was deeply unsympathetic to the women's cause.

In the early years of the 20th century a number of bills were proposed to grant women limited suffrage but all failed to become law. Then in 1910 the latest of these, the Conciliation Bill, which would have given a limited number of wealthy women the vote, was passed with a large majority. In the expectation that some women would soon be able to vote, the suffragettes suspended militant action. But this bill was dropped too. On 18 November, at the head of a deputation of suffragettes, Emmeline Pankhurst tried to enter the House of Commons to protest to Asquith about the dropping of the bill. When she was refused entry, her followers tried to break through the ring of police and force their way into Parliament. A riot broke out. Forced back by the police with exceptional brutality, the suffragettes named the day 'Black Friday'. It has been claimed that as many as two hundred women were arrested on this one day.

A further Conciliation Bill, proposed in 1912, was again sidelined. One of the problems was that many MPs feared that giving wealthy women the vote would only benefit the

Tory party. Others thought that there were more important things for Parliament to discuss. Many simply did not think that women should have the vote.

Women had gone to prison for the cause ever since 1905, when Christabel Pankhurst and Annie Kenney had been imprisoned in Manchester. Many of those imprisoned began to go on hunger strike. The Government's response was to permit forcible feeding, a barbaric practice which caused public outrage. To counter public sympathy for imprisoned suffragettes, in 1913 the government introduced a bill which became popularly known as the 'Cat and Mouse Act'. Under it, hunger-striking suffragette prisoners were released from prison on licence when their health deteriorated and arrested again when the licence expired. To escape re-arrest suffragette 'mice' went into hiding, protected by fellow suffragettes and other sympathizers. (Edith Key, the secretary of the Huddersfield WSPU, was one of those who helped shelter suffragette 'mice'.)

Suffragette militancy increased. To escape arrest for conspiracy, Christabel Pankhurst fled to Paris, where she continued to direct WSPU operations. Noisy protests were replaced by arson attacks on public property. Houses of public figures were burnt down, post boxes set alight, windows smashed, famous paintings destroyed. Although violence was never directed against a person these acts of vandalism swung public sympathy away from the suffragettes. Those men who dared to show support for the women's cause were treated roughly. On Derby Day, 1913, Emily Wilding Davison became the movement's first 'martyr' when she died of injuries following her attempt to seize the bridle of the King's horse as it galloped down Epsom racecourse.

In 1914 the First World War broke out. Immediately the suffragettes suspended their campaign, suffragette prisoners were released and suffragette leaders threw their support behind the war, calling on men to enlist. Meanwhile the NUWSS and some members of the WSPU encouraged women to take on the jobs vacated by the men and continued to press the cause of women's suffrage. In 1918, after the war had ended, the government passed the Representation of the People Act, which gave the vote to all men over 21 and to women over 30 who were householders, were married to householders, occupied property which had an annual rent of at least £5 (a lot of money in those days), or who were graduates of British universities.

It was the first step. On 2 July 1928, in the Equal Franchise Act, all women were finally given the vote on the same terms as men (those aged over 21). Sadly, Emmeline Pankhurst did not live to see the act became law. She had died a few weeks earlier, on 14 June. 41 years later, in 1969, the voting age for men and women in Britain was lowered to eighteen.

ACKNOWLEDGEMENTS

My grateful thanks to Jill Liddington, for putting me in contact with Dora's family, and whose book *Rebel Girls* (Virago Press) was the inspiration for *Give Us the Vote*.

I'd also like to acknowledge the assistance of the following people and organizations who have been so helpful locating documents, digging out archive material and trying to find answers to the unanswerable.

- The staff at Huddersfield's Local Studies library and the West Yorkshire Archive Service, especially Caroline Knight, Lynn McLean and Linda Hill
- Isabel Holland, project officer, Tolson Memorial Museum
- Chris Yeates, Museums Collections Officer, Kirklees Museums and Galleries
- Alan Brooke for sharing his exhaustive record of Huddersfield mills
- Beverley Cook, Curator, Social and Working History, the department of History Collections, Museum of London

- Professor Paul Ward, University of Huddersfield
- Hilary Haigh, archivist, University of Huddersfield
- Adam Carter, Bury library
- Staff at the Huddersfield Town Hall for kindly showing me around when the hall was closed

And finally I'd like to thank Dora's descendants – Chris Dow, Kerrie Bartholomew, Philip and Peter Carey – who as well as trying to answer my numerous questions so kindly shared with me memories and recollections of their grandmother.

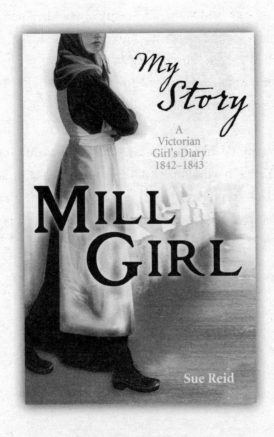

My Story

A Victorian Girl's Diary 1842–1843

MILL GIRL

Sue Reid

In spring 1842 Eliza is shocked when
she is sent to work in the Manchester cotton
mills – the noisy, suffocating mills. The work is
backbreaking and dangerous – and when she sees her
friends' lives wrecked by poverty, sickness
and unrest, Eliza realizes she must fight to escape
the fate of a mill girl...

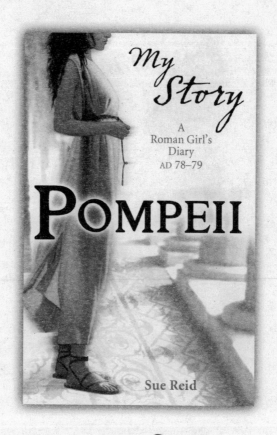

My Story

A
Roman Girl's
Diary
AD 78–79

POMPEII

Sue Reid

It's August AD 78 and Claudia is at
the Forum in Pompeii. It's a day of
strange encounters and even odder portents.
When the ground shakes Claudia is
convinced it is a bad omen. What does it all mean?
And why is she so disturbed by Vesuvius,
the great volcano that looms over the city...

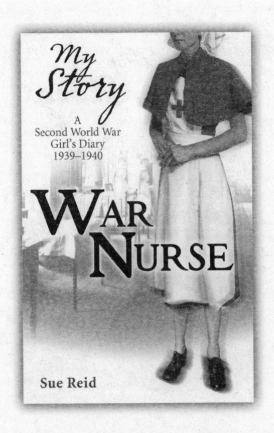

When **war breaks** out in **1939** **Kitty** signs up
to be a **Red Cross nurse** in a **military hospital**.
And it's not long before she's treating **badly**
wounded casualties from the war now **raging**
across Europe. Then the hospital takes a
direct hit and Kitty finds herself
a reluctant heroine...

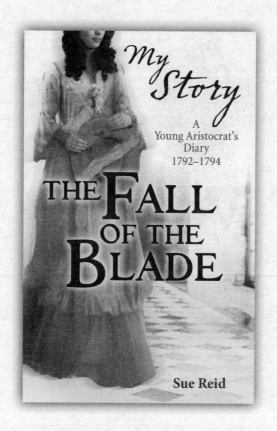

My Story

A
Young Aristocrat's
Diary
1792–1794

THE FALL
OF THE
BLADE

Sue Reid

It's 1792. Isabelle, daughter of an aristocrat,
lives in a chateau just outside Paris. But France
is in the grip of the Revolution, and as terror
takes hold of the city, Isabelle's family decide that
they must flee to the countryside.
But will they be safe there? Will they escape
the guillotine's falling blade...?

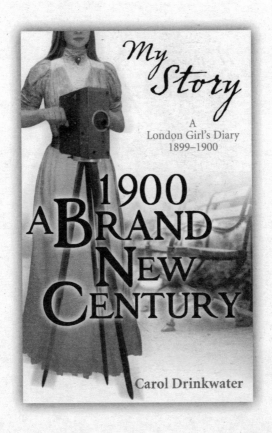

My Story

A
London Girl's Diary
1899–1900

1900
A BRAND
NEW
CENTURY

Carol Drinkwater

Christmas 1899. It's an exciting time to be **young;** the **twentieth century** is dawning. It's a **thrilling world** of new ideas, new possibilities and **new inventions –** phonographs, automobiles and **moving pictures...** Fourteen-year-old **Flora** is determined to take advantage of everything the new century **has to offer,** but how will she **persuade her** stuffy strait-laced father...

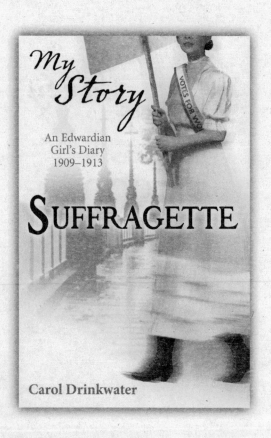

My *Story*

An Edwardian
Girl's Diary
1909–1913

SUFFRAGETTE

VOTES FOR WO[MEN]

Carol Drinkwater

It's 1909. Dollie is swept up in the thrill of
the campaign for Votes for Women. Against
her guardian's wishes, she marches against Parliament with
Emmeline Pankhurst and her fellow suffragettes.

But as the movement turns violent, women
are imprisoned and endanger their lives with hunger
strikes. Dollie must decide how far she will go for
'Deeds, not words'...